The Amaranthine Promises

A Journey of Love Lost and Found

RONAK SHAILESH BARVALIYA

Summary

"The Amaranthine Promises" is a tale of second chances, heartbreak, and the power of redemption. Kabir, a man once shattered by betrayal, finds himself at a crossroads between the remnants of his painful past and the possibility of a brighter future. After losing his first love, Maya, in a devastating breakup that left him questioning everything he once believed in, Kabir thought love was a chapter he could never reopen.

But when Siya enters his life, she brings with her the hope of healing and the promise of a love more profound than he ever imagined. As they navigate their journey together, Kabir is forced to confront the wounds of his past, the shadows of his regrets, and the strength it takes to love again.

"The Amaranthine Promises" follows the intricate tapestry of life showcasing how every action, every choice, leaves a permanent mark upon the fabric of existence. Betrayal, deceit, and the trials of fate may cast shadows upon our path, but it is the unwavering power of true love that illuminates the way forward.

Through the trials and tribulations of their journey, Kabir, Siya, and Maya come to understand the profound implications of karma—the universal law of cause and effect that governs the ebb and flow of human existence. They learn that every action carries consequences, and that true redemption lies in accepting responsibility for the choices we make.

Amidst the darkness of betrayal and the tumult of fate, a beacon of hope emerges—the transformative power of true love. Found in the unlikeliest of places and the most unexpected of moments, true love transcends the boundaries of time and space, offering solace in the face of adversity and strength amid chaos.

Through their journey, Kabir and Siya discover that love is not merely a fleeting emotion, but a profound force that binds together the threads of destiny. It is through the trials of betrayal and the challenges of karma that they come to realize the true depth of their love for one another, finding solace and redemption in each other's arms.

Contents

"I will never forget, and I will never forgive."

His words sliced through the air, sharp and final, leaving her frozen in the wake of his departure. As the door swung shut, she was left alone at the table, her hollow soul drowning in the silence he left behind.

But hang on, this is not a story about revenge…

Chapter 1
Mesmerized by a Mirage

The sun hung lazily in the sky, casting a warm glow over the busy college campus. Among the sea of students, one figure stood out - confident, charismatic, and utterly carefree. This was Kabir, a young man with a knack for dancing, a wicked sense of humour, and a smile that could light up even the gloomiest of days.

Kabir is a multifaceted individual, embodying qualities of love, care, and compassion in every aspect of his life. Born into a loving family, Kabir's early years are marked by moments of joy and innocence, his laughter echoing through the halls of his childhood home. Raised with values of kindness and empathy, he learns to navigate the world with an open heart and a generous spirit, forging deep connections with those around him. His kind-heartedness knows no bounds, as he effortlessly embodies the role of a trusted friend, offering a listening ear and a comforting presence to those in need. Despite his mischievous tendencies, Kabir never intends harm, preferring instead to spread happiness and positivity wherever he goes. With a heart as pure as a child's and a soul filled with boundless love, Kabir is like a bonfire in a world often shrouded in darkness, reminding us of the power of innocence, kindness, and unconditional love.

The Amaranthine Promises: Where love finds its way in the labyrinth of fate, illuminating the path to redemption and renewal. With each page turned, you may find solace in the power of forgiveness and boundless depths of true love.

As Kabir steps onto the sprawling campus of his college, he is greeted by a sight that takes his breath away—a verdant oasis of learning and discovery, where ivy-clad buildings stand in stately grandeur against a backdrop of lush greenery. Tall trees sway gently in the breeze, their leaves whispering secrets of generations past, while flower beds burst with vibrant blooms, painting the landscape with a riot of colour.

The classrooms, with their polished wooden floors and rows of desks bathed in warm sunlight streaming through large windows, are a haven of intellectual exploration. Here, students gather to engage in lively debates, delve into the depths of academic discourse, and cultivate the seeds of knowledge that will shape their futures. But it's not all about academics on campus—far from it. In the lively canteen, the air is filled with the tantalizing aroma of freshly brewed coffee and sizzling snacks, as students gather to refuel and recharge between classes. Laughter rings out as friends share stories and jokes, while the clatter of plates and cutlery adds to the lively atmosphere. Outside, on the college grounds, a sense of camaraderie and community prevails as students come together to participate in a myriad of extracurricular activities. From sports tournaments to cultural festivals, there is never a dull moment on campus, as students embrace the opportunity to pursue their passions and forge lasting friendships along the way.

In this vibrant and dynamic environment, Kabir finds himself immersed in a world of endless possibilities, where every corner holds the promise of new adventures and unforgettable experiences. As he navigates the halls of his college, he discovers not only the beauty of academia but also the richness of human connection and the joy of shared moments that will stay with him long after graduation.

Kabir steps into the animated canteen of his college, he notices a diverse group of students chatting and laughing together. Among them is Sarah, a bubbly and outgoing girl with a contagious laugh and a love for adventure. She's always the life of the party, organizing impromptu outings and cheering everyone up with her infectious energy. Next to Sarah sits Emily, a cheerful and chubby girl with a heart of gold. Emily exudes confidence and warmth, making her a beloved figure among her peers. She's known for her quick wit and sense of humour, always ready with a joke or a funny story to brighten someone's day. On the other side of the table is Riya, a dusky beauty with a flirtatious smile and a twinkle in her eye. She's the one who keeps the group entertained with her playful banter and sassy comebacks, always keeping everyone on their toes. Beside Riya is Chet, a simple-minded guy with a heart of gold who always seems to have a smile on his face. He's known for his kindness and willingness to help his friends, even if he doesn't always understand what's going on. Despite David's constant teasing and insistence, Chet never hesitates to foot the bill for the group, earning him the title of the "Canteen King."

As Kabir gets to know each of them better, he realizes that they all bring something unique to the table, whether it's Sarah's sense of adventure, Emily's infectious laughter, Riya's flirtatious charm, Chet's kindness, or David's mischievous pranks. Together, they form a tight-knit group of friends who support each other through the ups and downs of college life.

The college semester progresses, a new face appears in the busy hallways of the campus. Maya, with her quiet demeanour and reserved nature, seems to blend into the background amidst the chatter and excitement of her peers. Her arrival during the mid-term, a result of her father's work transfer, goes largely unnoticed by the student body, overshadowed by the bustling activity of college life. Maya's lack of confidence is evident in her hesitant movements and downcast gaze. She seems uncertain in her new surroundings, unsure of where she fits in among her classmates. Unlike the outgoing personalities that dominate the college landscape, Maya prefers to keep to herself, avoiding the spotlight whenever possible. Despite her reservations, Maya harbours a secret passion for celebrity culture, finding solace in the glamorous lives of the rich and famous. She spends her free time scrolling through social media feeds, silently observing the lives of her favourite stars from afar. In the world of celebrity gossip, Maya finds a temporary escape from her own insecurities, losing herself in the drama and excitement of a world far removed from her own. While Maya may not possess the confidence or charisma of her more outspoken peers, her quiet presence adds a unique depth to the college atmosphere. Beneath her shy exterior lies a world of hidden potential and untapped passion, waiting to be discovered by those who take the time to look beyond the surface.

One fine day as Kabir strolled through the campus, his eyes caught sight of this girl standing by the water cooler.

The Amaranthine Promises: Where love finds its way in the labyrinth of fate, illuminating the path to redemption and renewal. With each page turned, you may find solace in the power of forgiveness and boundless depths of true love.

Time seemed to slow as he took in her beauty - her radiant smile, her flowing hair, the sparkle in her eyes. In that instant, he was mesmerized.

With a casual swagger, Kabir approached the girl, offering her a charming grin. "Mind if I join you?" he asked, gesturing towards the cooler. The girl glanced up, startled by his sudden appearance. But her surprise quickly melted into a warm smile. "Sure, go ahead," she replied, making room for him. And just like that, a friendship was born. As the days passed, Maya found herself drawn to a group of students who frequented the college canteen, led by the charismatic Kabir. Despite her initial reservations, Maya was welcomed into the fold with open arms, her quiet presence adding a new dimension to the dynamic of the group.

As Maya became more comfortable with her newfound friends, she gravitated towards Sarah, a fellow member of the group whose easy-going nature and warm smile instantly put her at ease. The two bonded over shared interests and inside jokes, forging a friendship that would soon become an integral part of Maya's college experience. Meanwhile, Kabir found himself building a strong bond with David, the mischievous prankster of the group whose infectious laughter and playful tricks never failed to brighten the mood. From impromptu football matches in the college park to late-night study sessions at the library that often devolved into laughter-filled escapades, Kabir and David became inseparable, their friendship growing stronger with each passing day.

Weeks turned into months and the bonds between Maya, Sarah, Kabir, and David deepened, their shared experiences at the canteen and around campus creating a sense of solidarity that transcended mere friendship. Together, they navigated the ups and downs of college life, supporting each other through the challenges and celebrating the triumphs, creating memories that would last a lifetime. Over the coming days, Kabir and Maya grew closer. They sat together in class, shared jokes and stories, and quickly became the best of friends.

But within the laughter and amity, Kabir couldn't shake the feeling that there was something more between him and Maya. He found himself drawn to her in ways he couldn't quite understand, his thoughts constantly drifting to her whenever they were apart. Amidst the vibrant campus events, Maya's beauty was like a rare and exquisite flower blooming amidst a field of wildflowers. Her allure was undeniable, drawing the gaze of all who crossed her path. Despite her captivating beauty, Maya's dedication to her studies and her involvement in college events was equally remarkable. She approached every task with a steadfast determination and an unwavering commitment, leaving an indelible impression on those around her.

Soon Kabir started working alongside Maya, he couldn't help but be enchanted by her magnetic presence. Her beauty was like a spell, weaving its way into his heart, and yet it was her dedication and passion that truly captivated him. With each passing day, Kabir found himself falling deeper under Maya's enchanting spell, his admiration blossoming into something more profound and undeniable. It was the little things that caught his attention—the gentle touch of their hands as they shared a pen to jot down notes in class, the way her laughter echoed through the halls of the college, the sparkle in her eyes when she spoke about her passions and dreams. Days turned into weeks and the weeks into months, Kabir's feelings for Maya only grew stronger. Despite his best efforts to ignore the growing feelings stirring within him, Kabir couldn't deny the magnetic pull he felt towards Maya. She was unlike anyone he had ever met before, her quiet strength and unwavering determination captivating him in ways he never thought possible. He found himself fantasizing about what it would be like to hold her hand, to feel her lips against his, to be more than just friends.

One fine morning Kabir and Maya were engrossed in their conversation at the college canteen, a new figure entered the scene. Jake, Kabir's friend, sauntered over with a confident grin, his eyes immediately drawn to Maya's presence. "Hey there, Maya," Jake greeted with a charming smile, leaning casually against the nearby table. "You're looking even more stunning than usual today." Maya laughed lightly, batting her eyelashes playfully. "Flattery will get you nowhere, Jake," she replied, but her smile betrayed a hint of amusement. Kabir couldn't help but notice the subtle exchange between his friend and Maya, feeling a pang of jealousy tugging at his heart. He cleared his throat, trying to refocus the conversation back to their group's activities for the day. Despite his growing infatuation, Kabir couldn't bring himself to confess his feelings to Maya. Instead, he watched helplessly as she developed a crush on his friend, Jake the fair skinned charmer with striking green eyes.

The next day as Jake approached, Maya's eyes lit up with a mischievous glint. "Hey, Jake," she greeted, her tone playful.

"You're looking rather dashing today yourself." Kabir felt a twinge of discomfort at the exchange, but Maya seemed unfazed as she continued, "Kabir, isn't it fascinating how Jake always manages to make an entrance?" Kabir forced a smile, trying to 11 "Yeah, he's got a knack for it," he replied tersely, shooting a subtle glance at Maya, hoping she'd pick up on his discomfort. But Maya simply shrugged, flashing Jake a teasing grin. "So, Jake, what brings you over here today? Planning on sweeping another unsuspecting soul off their feet?" Jake chuckled, shooting a playful wink at Maya. "Just couldn't resist the chance to brighten your day with my charming presence," he quipped, earning a playful swat from Maya. Kabir sighed inwardly, feeling increasingly out of place amidst the banter. He silently wished for a way to steer the conversation back to safer ground, away from the flirtatious undertones that seemed to hang in the air.

As the flirtatious banter between Jake and Maya continued, Kabir felt a surge of resentment building within him. Each playful exchange, each teasing smile exchanged between them, felt like a dagger twisting in his heart. He struggled to maintain a facade of nonchalance, but inside, a storm was brewing. The laughter that filled the air grated on his nerves, fuelling the fire of jealousy that burned within him. Despite his best efforts to ignore it, the growing closeness between Maya and Jake gnawed at him relentlessly. He couldn't shake the feeling of being side-lined, of being the outsider looking in on a world where he no longer belonged. And soon Maya found herself caught in dreams of a whirlwind romance with

Jake, he seemed to embody everything she had ever dreamed of in a partner.

As Maya's friendship with Jake blossomed, Kabir couldn't help but feel a stitch of jealousy deep within his chest. He knew he had no right to feel this way, he had no claim over her heart. But try as he might, he couldn't shake the feeling that perhaps, just perhaps, there could be something more between them. Caught between his growing feelings for Maya and his desire to see her happy, Kabir found himself at a crossroads, unsure of which path to take. Should he continue to suppress his feelings and support Maya in winning over Jake's love, or should he take a chance and confess his love, risking their friendship in the process?

Days passed and Kabir grappled with his emotions, one thing became clear—he couldn't deny the depth of his feelings for Maya any longer. Whether or not she felt the same way remained to be seen, but one thing was certain—Kabir was willing to take the risk, no matter the outcome. However, the realization hit Kabir like a punch to the gut. Here he was, head over heels for Maya, while she pined away for someone else. It was a bitter pill to swallow, one that left him feeling hollow and defeated. And as the truth of Maya's feelings for his friend sank in, Kabir's heart hardened with a bitter mixture of betrayal and resentment.

The once warm and affectionate connection he had shared with Maya now turned cold and distant, replaced by a simmering disdain that threatened to consume him. With each passing day, Kabir found himself consumed by a growing sense of resentment towards Maya. The very sight of her filled him with a seething anger, a stark reminder of the pain and humiliation she had inflicted upon him. Gone was the tenderness he had once felt towards her, replaced by a cold and unyielding animosity that burned like a flame within his soul. In his bitterness, Kabir began to distance himself from Maya, cutting off all contact and avoiding her presence whenever possible. He refused to acknowledge her existence, turning a deaf ear to her attempts at reconciliation and closure. Every interaction with her was met with icy silence, a soundless condemnation of her actions and the hurt she had caused him.

One such incident occurred during a college event where Maya, accustomed to Kabir's unwavering support in the past, turned to him for assistance in organizing a crucial aspect of the program. In the midst of the college event planning, Maya eagerly turned to Kabir, her eyes bright with excitement. "Hey, Kabir, we could really use your help with organizing the decorations. What do you think?" Kabir hesitated, a flicker of discomfort crossing his features. "Um, actually, Maya, I think I'll pass on this one. I've got a lot on my plate right now." Maya's smile faltered slightly, confusion knitting her brows together. "But Kabir, you've always been so involved in these events. Is everything okay?" Kabir forced a tight smile, masking the turmoil brewing beneath the surface. "Yeah, everything's fine. I just... I've got other stuff to take care of." Maya's expression softened, concern glinting in her eyes. "Are you sure? You know you can talk to me if something's bothering you." But Kabir brushed off her offer with a dismissive wave of his hand. "I'm sure. Thanks, Maya. I'll catch you later." With that, he turned and walked away, leaving Maya standing there, her heart heavy with unanswered questions. In a display of his newfound antipathy towards her, Kabir declined her request with a curt refusal, leaving Maya stunned and bewildered by his sudden change in attitude. Thereafter, despite Maya's attempts to salvage their fractured relationship, Kabir remained resolute in his decision to distance himself from her, refusing to offer even a modicum of assistance or emotional support.

As time passed, Kabir's hatred for Maya only grew stronger, festering like a wound that refused to heal. He found himself consumed by thoughts of revenge, fantasizing about the day when he would have the opportunity to make her pay for her betrayal. Yet, deep down, he knew that his anger was a reflection of his own pain and wounded pride, a futile attempt to mask the heartbreak that still lingered within him.

Despite his best efforts to move on, Kabir's hatred for Maya remained a constant presence in his life, a bitter reminder of the love that had turned to ashes. And though he knew that forgiveness was the path to healing, he couldn't bring himself to let go of the anger that consumed him, trapped in a cycle of resentment and bitterness that threatened to consume him whole. Kabir found himself unable to muster even a semblance of support for her, a stark departure from his usual demeanour of kindness and empathy. In every interaction, he made it abundantly clear that he no longer had any intention of being there for her, his actions speaking volumes in their silent condemnation.

His indifference cut Maya to the core, a painful reminder of the rift that had formed between them and the irreparable damage that had been done to their once close bond. Maya struggled to come to terms with Kabir's cold rejection, she was forced to confront the harsh reality that their friendship had been irreparably cleft by her own actions. In Kabir's steadfast refusal to offer her any semblance of kindness or compassion, she saw a reflection of the pain and hurt she had inflicted upon him, a bitter reminder of the consequences of her betrayal. For Kabir, each refusal to support Maya served as a form of catharsis, a way to channel his anger and resentment towards her into tangible action. Yet, even as he stood firm in his decision to distance himself from her, he couldn't shake the lingering ache in his heart, a silent testament to the depth of the bond that had once existed between them.

But, as he withdrew, something unexpected happened. Maya, sensing his growing distance, began to panic. She realized, too late, that she had taken Kabir for granted, that her feelings for him ran deeper than she had ever dared to admit. In the midst of her turmoil, Maya found herself haunted by memories of the genuine connection she had shared with Kabir, a bond forged through laughter, shared dreams, and whispered confidences. As she reflected on their time together, she realized with a jolt of clarity that her feelings for Jake were nothing more than a fleeting distraction, a temporary escape from the painful truth she had been unwilling to acknowledge.

With each passing day, Maya's heart ached with longing for the warmth and affection she had once found in Kabir's presence. The walls she had built around her heart crumbled in the face of the overwhelming tide of emotions that threatened to engulf her, leaving her vulnerable and exposed to the raw intensity of her true feelings. As Maya sat alone in her room, her thoughts consumed by all the recent events, she found herself engaged in an unexpected conversation. It wasn't with a friend or a family member, but rather with her own heart.

Heart: Maya, are you really happy with the way things are going between you and Kabir?

Maya paused, taken aback by the sudden question from within. "Of course, I am," she replied, though the uncertainty in her voice betrayed her true feelings.

Heart: Really? Because lately, I've been feeling like something's missing. Like we're drifting apart.

Maya frowned, a pang of guilt tugging at her conscience. "We're just going through a rough patch. It'll pass," she reasoned, though her heart remained unconvinced.

Heart: But what if it doesn't? What if we're letting something truly special slip away because we're too afraid to confront the truth?

Maya's brow furrowed as she mulled over her heart's words. "I don't know, maybe you're right," she admitted, her voice barely above a whisper.

Heart: Maya, don't ignore what you're feeling. Listen to me, and let's find a way to make things right before it's too late.

In a moment of clarity, Maya's heart spoke the words her lips had been too afraid to utter, confessing the depth of her love for Kabir with a fervour that shook her to the core. It was a revelation that filled her with both fear and exhilaration, a brave acknowledgment of the love she had been too blind to see until now. Maya grappled with the magnitude of her

The Amaranthine Promises: Where love finds its way in the labyrinth of fate, illuminating the path to redemption and renewal. With each page turned, you may find solace in the power of forgiveness and boundless depths of true love.

newfound realization, she knew that she had to find the courage to confront Kabir and lay bare the truth of her heart. For in his eyes, she saw the reflection of her own longing, a silent plea for forgiveness and redemption that echoed the depths of her soul. With a heavy sigh, Maya closed her eyes, finally allowing herself to acknowledge the doubts and fears that had been festering within. Perhaps it was time to confront the truth and take a leap of faith, no matter how uncertain the outcome may be.

And so, with trembling hands and a heart full of hope, Maya took the first tentative steps towards reconciliation. But, with a heavy heart, Maya retreated every single time with Kabir's cold rejection, the sting of his cruel words echoing in her mind like a relentless refrain, "sorry I am busy", "No I am not interested", "can't make it" and on and on. Despite her best efforts to steel herself against the pain, she found herself consumed by a suffocating sense of despair, her hopes dashed against the jagged rocks of Kabir's indifference.

In the depths of her anguish, Maya clung to the fragile threads of her resolve, determined to find a way to bridge the chasm that had opened between them. With each passing day, she wrestled with her inner demons, grappling with the torment of unrequited love and the relentless ache of longing that threatened to consume her whole. Unable to muster the courage to confess her true feelings to Kabir face-to-face, it was in the quiet solitude of her despair that Maya devised a desperate plan, a last-ditch effort to lay bare the truth of her heart in a way that words alone could not convey. With quivering hands, she carefully transcribed the depths of her

The Amaranthine Promises: Where love finds its way in the labyrinth of fate, illuminating the path to redemption and renewal. With each page turned, you may find solace in the power of forgiveness and boundless depths of true love.

emotions onto the pristine pages of her diary, detailing every fleeting glance, every whispered conversation, and every stolen moment shared between them. As she poured her soul onto the blank canvas of the pages, Maya felt a glimmer of hope flicker to life within her.

With each stroke of her pen, she bared her soul to the one who held her heart captive, laying unadorned the raw intensity of her love in a silent plea for understanding and acceptance. With her heart laid bare for all to see, Maya left her diary behind, a silent testament to the depth of her devotion and the unwavering strength of her love. Though she knew not whether Kabir would ever read her words, she found solace in the knowledge that she had revealed her soul to him in the only way she knew how, leaving the rest to fate's capricious hand.

And so it was that Kabir, alone in his room one evening, stumbled upon Maya's diary. Kabir wrestled with his conscience, the temptation to read Maya's diary loomed large in his mind like an overripe fruit begging to be plucked. He knew it was wrong, like sneaking an extra cookie from the jar when no one was looking, but the allure was irresistible. As Kabir hesitated, his conscience spoke up, urging him to reconsider his actions.

Conscience: Kabir, you know it's not right to invade Maya's privacy like this. Reading her diary is a breach of trust, and you'll only end up hurting her if she finds out.

Kabir shifted uncomfortably, torn between his desire to uncover the truth and the nagging guilt of betraying Maya's trust. "But what if there's something important in here? Something that could explain everything?" he reasoned, though his conscience remained unconvinced.

Conscience: Even if there is, Kabir, it's not your place to pry into Maya's personal thoughts and feelings. Trust is the foundation of any relationship, and you're risking everything by going against it.

With a heavy sigh, Kabir closed his eyes, wrestling with the internal conflict raging within. In the end, curiosity got the better of him, and he reluctantly opened the diary, steeling himself for whatever revelations lay within. Kabir tiptoed to where Maya had left her diary, feeling like a clumsy cat attempting a stealthy approach to the prize. With trembling hands, he gingerly picked up the diary, half expecting it to emit a warning growl or sprout wings and fly away.

Curiosity piqued, he flipped through its pages, his heart pounding in his chest as he read her words of longing, of regret, of love. As Kabir reluctantly leafed through the pages of Maya's diary, he was unprepared for the torrent of emotions that would come crashing down upon him like a tidal wave. With each word, each confession laid bare in stark relief upon the page, he felt the icy tendrils of hatred that had encased his heart begin to thaw, melting away in the searing heat of Maya's unbridled passion.

As Kabir read of her feelings, her hopes, and her dreams, Kabir found himself transported back to a time when Friendship had blossomed between them like a fragile flower in the harsh light of day. He remembered the laughter they had shared, the whispered confidences exchanged beneath the moonlit sky, and the promises of forever that had once flowed freely from their lips. The heft of Maya's words settled upon him like a heavy burden, Kabir felt a profound sense of remorse pouring down on him, drowning out the echoes of his anger and resentment. He realized the extent of the pain he had caused, the depth of the wounds he had inflicted upon Maya's tender heart, and the irrevocable damage his actions had wrought upon their once-cherished bond.

Conscience: Kabir, do you see this? Maya has poured her heart out in these pages. She loves you, truly and deeply.

Kabir's hands trembled slightly as he processed the magnitude of Maya's confession. Could it be true? After all the pain and heartache, was there still a chance for them to be together?

Conscience: It's time to set things right, Kabir. You've been holding back for too long, letting fear and doubt cloud your judgment. But Maya's feelings are clear as day, and it's up to you to seize this opportunity.

Kabir: You're right. It's time to stop running away from my feelings and confront them head-on. Maya deserves to know the truth, and I'm going to tell her exactly how I feel.

With determination in his eyes, Kabir closed the diary and made a silent vow to make things right with Maya once and for all. It was time to take a leap of faith and follow his heart. In that moment, everything became clear. Maya was not just a friend, not just a crush - she was the one he had been searching

The Amaranthine Promises: Where love finds its way in the labyrinth of fate, illuminating the path to redemption and renewal. With each page turned, you may find solace in the power of forgiveness and boundless depths of true love.

for all along. And so, with trembling hands and a racing heart, Kabir made a decision. It was time to lay his cards on the table and tell Maya how he truly felt.

In the opening chapter of "The Amaranthine Promises," we are introduced to Kabir, a young person whose life is forever altered by a chance encounter with Maya, a captivating vision of beauty amidst the mundane landscape of their college campus. As Kabir finds himself inexplicably drawn to Maya's enigmatic presence, they embark on a journey of discovery, navigating the intricacies of love and desire in the shadow of a fleeting mirage.

The Amaranthine Promises: Where love finds its way in the labyrinth of fate, illuminating the path to redemption and renewal. With each page turned, you may find solace in the power of forgiveness and boundless depths of true love.

Chapter 2
Firelight Revelations

With Maya's diary still clutched tightly in his hand, Kabir felt a surge of determination coursing through his veins. With each passing moment, as he delved deeper into the recesses of Maya's soul, Kabir felt the walls around his heart crumble, the barriers he had erected against her love falling away like dust in the wind. In their place, he felt a wellspring of compassion and understanding bubble to the surface, filling him with an overwhelming desire to make amends for the pain he had caused. And so, with tears streaming down his cheeks and Maya's diary grasped firmly in his trembling hands, Kabir made a solemn vow to right the wrongs of the past, to seek forgiveness for his transgressions, and to rebuild the shattered remnants of their fractured love from the ashes of their pain. He knew what he had to do - he had to tell Maya how he felt, no matter the outcome.

Summoning every ounce of courage he possessed, Kabir sought out Maya, his heart pounding with anticipation. Kabir stepped into the hushed confines of the college library, the familiar scent of old books and dust filled his senses, wrapping him in a cocoon of quiet contemplation. Rows of shelves stretched out before him, laden with volumes of knowledge and secrets waiting to be discovered, while shafts of golden sunlight filtered through the windows, casting dappled patterns

The Amaranthine Promises: Where love finds its way in the labyrinth of fate, illuminating the path to redemption and renewal. With each page turned, you may find solace in the power of forgiveness and boundless depths of true love.

of light and shadow upon the polished wooden floors. Amidst this tranquil scene, Kabir's gaze fell upon Maya, seated at a small table tucked away in a secluded corner of the library. She was lost in thought, her brow furrowed in concentration as she poured over the pages of a thick tome, her fingers tracing the lines of text with a delicate touch.

As Kabir approached, his footsteps echoing softly in the hallowed halls of the library, he felt a knot of apprehension tighten in his chest. This was it, the moment he had been dreading and yet longing for in equal measure. With each step closer to Maya's table, he felt the burden of his confession grow heavier upon his shoulders, the words he had rehearsed a thousand times over now catching in his throat like shards of broken glass. But as he finally reached her side, "Maya," he began, his voice steady despite the turmoil within, "there's something I need to tell you." Maya looked up, "What is it, Kabir?" her eyes alight with curiosity and surprise. There was a vulnerability in her gaze, a flicker of uncertainty beneath the surface of her outward composure, that gave Kabir pause. Kabir saw her not as the object of his resentment or the source of his pain, but as a fellow traveller upon the winding path of life, navigating the twists and turns with courage and grace.

Taking a seat beside her, Kabir took her hand in his, his fingers trembling slightly. "I...I read your diary," he admitted, his cheeks flushing with embarrassment. "I know I shouldn't have, but I couldn't help myself." He braced himself for her reaction, his heart pounding in his chest with a mixture of anticipation and apprehension. But to his surprise, Maya's response was not one of anger or betrayal, but of understanding

The Amaranthine Promises: Where love finds its way in the labyrinth of fate, illuminating the path to redemption and renewal. With each page turned, you may find solace in the power of forgiveness and boundless depths of true love.

and acceptance. For a moment, Maya's expression remained unreadable, her gaze searching his face for signs of deceit. But then, to Kabir's relief, a small grin tugged at the corners of her lips. With a gentle smile, Maya reached out to take Kabir's hand in hers, her touch sending a rush of warmth flooding through his veins. "It's okay, Kabir," she said softly, her voice a soothing melody that splashed over him like a summer breeze. "I wanted you to read it."

The admission caught Kabir off guard, his mind reeling with disbelief. "You...you wanted me to read it?" a sense of relief flooding through him like a tide. He had feared that Maya would be angry or hurt by his actions, but instead, she offered him forgiveness and understanding, her eyes shining with a tenderness that filled him with a sense of wonder. Unable to contain his feelings any longer, Kabir reached out to pull Maya into his arms, holding her close as he buried his face in the crook of her neck. "Thank you," he whispered, his voice thick with emotion. "Thank you for understanding, for forgiving me." Maya hugged him back tightly, her arms wrapping around him in a gesture of comfort and reassurance. "There's nothing to forgive," she murmured, her words a gentle caress against his ear. Maya nodded, her smile widening. "Yes. I left it behind on purpose, hoping that you would find it and understand how I feel." They sat together in the embrace of the library, Kabir knew that he had found something precious and rare in Maya's compassion. a second chance at love, a chance to start over and build something beautiful together.

In that moment, everything fell into place. The walls that had stood between them crumbled away, leaving only honesty

The Amaranthine Promises: Where love finds its way in the labyrinth of fate, illuminating the path to redemption and renewal. With each page turned, you may find solace in the power of forgiveness and boundless depths of true love.

and vulnerability in their wake. Kabir knew that this was the perfect moment to lay bare his heart before Maya. With a nervous yet determined energy coursing through his veins, he took a deep breath and dropped to one knee, the load of his love and devotion heavy in the air around them. "Maya," he began, his voice filled with a raw emotion that he could no longer contain, "from the moment I first saw you, I knew that you were something special. You've brought light into my life, chased away the darkness, and shown me what it means to truly love and be loved. I love you, Maya," Kabir whispered, his voice barely above a whisper. "I've loved you since the moment I laid eyes on you, and I can't imagine my life without you."

Maya's breath caught in her throat as she watched Kabir, her heart pounding in rhythm with his words. She had never seen him so vulnerable, so open and honest about his feelings, and it touched her in a way that words could not express. "Every moment with you has been a gift, Maya," Kabir continued, his eyes never leaving hers. "And I can't imagine spending the rest of my life with anyone else but you. Will you do me the honour of being my partner, my confidante, my love, for all eternity?" Tears welled up in Maya's eyes as she listened to Kabir's heartfelt confession, her heart overflowing with love and gratitude for the man before her. Without a moment's hesitation, she stepped forward and knelt down beside him, taking his hands in hers.

"Yes, Kabir," she whispered, her voice trembling with emotion. "A thousand times yes. I will be yours, now and forever." she said, her voice choked with tears. "I've loved you

The Amaranthine Promises: Where love finds its way in the labyrinth of fate, illuminating the path to redemption and renewal. With each page turned, you may find solace in the power of forgiveness and boundless depths of true love.

for so long, but I was afraid to admit it." With tears streaming down their cheeks, Kabir and Maya wrapped their arms around each other in a tight embrace, sealing their love and commitment with a kiss that spoke volumes of the depth of their connection. Surrounded by the beauty of the setting sun and the promise of a future filled with love and happiness, they knew that they had found their forever in each other's arms - two hearts, united in love and bound by destiny.

From that day forward, Kabir and Maya were inseparable. Every moment seemed to sparkle with the magic of newfound love. From flirtatious glances across the lecture hall to secret rendezvous in between classes, they found joy in the simplest of gestures and the quiet moments shared between them. They laughed together, cried together, and embarked on countless adventures that would shape the course of their lives. Their relationship blossomed into something beautiful, a love story for the ages. They celebrated milestones together - anniversaries, birthdays, and everything in between - each moment more precious than the last. They explored new heights of intimacy and shared countless memories together. From romantic dinners by candlelight to moonlit strolls under the stars, Kabir and Maya reveled in each other's company, their laughter ringing out like music in the night.

But it wasn't all smooth sailing for the young couple, as they navigated the ups and downs of love with equal parts grace and humour. There were moments of misunderstanding and miscommunication, of course, but they always found a way to laugh it off and come back stronger than ever. One particularly memorable evening, Kabir decided to surprise

Maya with tickets to her favourite movie, only to discover that she had already made plans with her friends. Undeterred, Kabir tagged along with Maya and her friends, turning what could have been an awkward situation into a hilarious night of laughter and camaraderie. Then there was the time when Maya accidentally spilled coffee all over Kabir's favourite shirt, prompting a mad dash to the nearest store to find a replacement. What started as a frantic search turned into an impromptu fashion show, as Kabir tried on shirt after shirt, much to Maya's amusement.

But perhaps the most memorable moment of all came when Kabir and Maya finally decided to reveal their relationship to their friends. With nerves tingling and hearts racing, they gathered their gang together for a special announcement, only to be met with cheers, applause, and a few playful jabs from their closest confidants. In the end, Kabir and Maya realized that love wasn't just about grand gestures and romantic gestures, but about the everyday moments shared between two.

Kabir's life had become intertwined with Maya's in ways he never imagined possible. Every decision he made, every choice he considered, was coloured by her presence, her desires, her dreams. From the smallest of daily routines to the grandest of plans for the future, Maya's influence loomed large over Kabir's life. Even his relationships with his college gang, once a source of joy and companionship, began to strain under the weight of Maya's demands on his time and attention. As their outings and gatherings became fewer and farther between,

Kabir found himself increasingly isolated from the friends who had once been like family to him.

At first, Kabir tried to juggle his commitments to Maya and his loyalty to his friends, but as Maya's expectations grew and their relationship deepened, he found himself making excuses, cancelling plans, and prioritizing her needs above all else. The once-close bond he shared with his college gang began to fray as they watched him drift further and further away, replaced by the constant presence of Maya in his life. And as the divide between Kabir and his friends widened, he couldn't help but feel a wrench of regret for the connections he had let slip away in favour of Maya's company. But in the grip of love's intoxicating embrace, he pushed aside his doubts and fears, convinced that sacrificing everything for Maya was worth any cost.

Kabir's dedication to Maya knew no bounds. In the quiet hours of the night and the early light of dawn, he would steal away from the confines of his home to find a private corner where he could call her, just to hear the sound of her voice and feel the warmth of her presence, if only through the phone. His tastes and preferences began to mirror hers as he sought to anticipate her every desire and whim, forsaking his own cravings and inclinations in favour of whatever brought Maya pleasure. The foods he once enjoyed fell by the wayside, replaced by her favourites, chosen with care and affection in the hopes of eliciting a smile or a word of thanks.

Even his relationships with his closest friends and family began to suffer as he redirected his time and energy toward Maya's happiness. Cricket matches with school friends were

---

The Amaranthine Promises: Where love finds its way in the labyrinth of fate, illuminating the path to redemption and renewal. With each page turned, you may find solace in the power of forgiveness and boundless depths of true love.

---

skipped, outings with his brother were postponed, and family dinners became a rare occurrence as Kabir devoted himself entirely to Maya's needs and wishes. And yet, despite the sacrifices he made and the compromises he endured, Kabir found a sense of fulfilment in the simple act of making Maya happy. Her laughter, her smiles, her moments of joy became his guiding light, driving him to greater lengths and deeper depths in his quest to keep her content and cared for.

Kabir's obsession with Maya had blinded him to the concerns of those closest to him, including his own brother. When his younger sibling confronted him, urging him to carve out time for friends and family, Kabir reacted with anger and defensiveness, unable to see the validity of his brother's words. Instead of recognizing the wisdom in his brother's advice, Kabir dismissed it as an unwarranted intrusion, viewing any suggestion that he should prioritize anything above Maya's happiness as a personal affront. In his mind, Maya's needs came first, above all else, and anyone who dared to suggest otherwise was met with hostility and resentment.

As Kabir's devotion to Maya grew, his relationships outside of their bubble began to wither. His college gang, once a tight-knit group of friends, gradually distanced themselves from him, feeling neglected and overlooked in favor of Kabir's singular focus on Maya. There was an incident at a college party where Kabir, usually the life of the gathering, found himself alone in a corner, nursing a drink and absentmindedly scrolling through his phone, waiting for a message from Maya. His friends, noticing his detachment, attempted to engage him in conversation and include him in the festivities, but Kabir's mind was elsewhere, his attention consumed by thoughts of Maya. Weeks passed, and invitations to hang out or attend events with his friends went unanswered as Kabir prioritized his time with Maya above all else. His friends, feeling rejected and unimportant, gradually stopped reaching out, resigning themselves to the reality that Kabir was no longer the friend they once knew.

But as the years passed, Kabir and Maya's once-perfect relationship began to show signs of strain. What had once been a bond forged in love and shared dreams now seemed fragile, as Maya's obsession with wealth and fame began to overshadow everything else. No matter how hard Kabir tried, it seemed like nothing he did could ever please Maya anymore. Her ambitions had grown larger than life, and she was no longer content with the simple joys of their life together. Instead, she constantly chased after the next big opportunity, the next chance for fame and fortune. For Maya, money had become the ultimate goal, the driving force behind every decision she made. She no longer seemed tied to any emotion or relationship, except for the allure of wealth. Her dreams soared higher and higher, leaving Kabir feeling like nothing more than a burden, a chain weighing her down.

Secretly, Maya began applying for jobs in far-off cities, her sights set on escaping their small town and the struggles of everyday life. She longed for the easy money and glamorous lifestyle she believed awaited her elsewhere, and she seemed willing to leave everything behind to chase her dreams. Meanwhile, Kabir felt like he was caught in a trap, his love for Maya turning into a heavy burden he couldn't shake

The Amaranthine Promises: Where love finds its way in the labyrinth of fate, illuminating the path to redemption and renewal. With each page turned, you may find solace in the power of forgiveness and boundless depths of true love.

off. He watched helplessly as she grew more distant, more consumed by her ambitions, until it felt like they were living in two different worlds. Despite his best efforts to hold their relationship together, Kabir couldn't ignore the growing rift between them. And as Maya's obsession with wealth and fame threatened to tear them apart, he began to wonder if their love was strong enough to survive the storm. In spite of the growing distance between them, Kabir refused to give up on the love he had once shared with Maya. He poured his heart and soul into trying to recapture the magic they had once shared, planning surprises, showering her with gifts, and showing her affection at every opportunity.

One particular moment stands out in Kabir's memory—a moment when he had excitedly bought two tickets to a concert, eager to surprise Maya and spend a memorable evening together. But instead of the joyous reaction he had hoped for, Maya's response was one of anger and frustration. She lashed out at Kabir, accusing him of overstepping boundaries and planning without her permission. It was a stark departure from the happy, carefree Maya he had once known. Despite his best efforts, Maya seemed to grow increasingly restless and dissatisfied with their relationship. Her oncebright eyes now held a shadow of discontent, and her laughter no longer rang as freely as it once had. Each failed attempt to reconnect with her left Kabir feeling a deep sense of sadness and helplessness, as he watched the love, they had shared slip further and further away.

Finally, the day came, Maya received the offer from the city of her dreams, her eyes sparkled with excitement and anticipation. It was an opportunity she had been dreaming of—a chance to pursue her ambitions and make a name for herself in the world. Without hesitation, she accepted the offer, her heart already soaring with visions of success and accomplishment. For Maya, the prospect of moving to a new city represented the fulfilment of her deepest desires.

As Maya danced around her room, her laughter echoing off the walls, she seemed to be oblivious to the sadness and hurt that clouded Kabir's heart. For him, Maya's decision to leave felt like a treachery—a betrayal of the love they had shared and the dreams they had once held together. But Maya's excitement was infectious, and Kabir found himself unable to dampen her spirits, even as his own heart broke at the thought of losing her. In the midst of Maya's excitement and joy, Kabir couldn't shake the feeling that their relationship was slipping away from him, like sand through his fingers. The announcement of Maya's job offer had hit Kabir like a tidal wave. They were sitting on the old, worn-out bench in the park, the same place where they had shared so many dreams and secrets. The soft glow of the streetlights cast long shadows, reflecting the turmoil in Kabir's heart.

Kabir: "Maya, I can't believe you're leaving. How can you just go? What about us?"

Maya sighed, her eyes reflecting a mixture of frustration and determination.

Maya: "Kabir, this is my chance to make something of myself. To follow my dreams. Don't you want that for me?"

The Amaranthine Promises: Where love finds its way in the labyrinth of fate, illuminating the path to redemption and renewal. With each page turned, you may find solace in the power of forgiveness and boundless depths of true love.

Kabir: "Of course I do, but… why can't you do that here? Why does it have to be so far away?"

Maya took a deep breath, her voice turning softer but carrying a manipulative edge.

Maya: "Kabir, think about it. This job is a steppingstone. A way to build a future for us. But I need you to support me, not hold me back. I thought you believed in me."

Kabir: "I do, but—"

Maya: "Then why are you making this so hard? I need you to be my rock, Kabir. To stand by me, not drag me down. Can't you see that this is what's best for both of us in the long run?"

Kabir's heart twisted painfully. He wanted to believe her, to support her dreams, but the thought of losing her was unbearable.

Kabir: "I don't want to lose you, Maya."

Maya's expression softened, her hand reaching out to gently touch his cheek. "You won't lose me. This is just a temporary distance. And when I come back, we'll be stronger than ever. But for that, I need you to let me go now. Please, Kabir, trust me on this."

Kabir looked into her eyes, searching for a hint of doubt but finding none. Reluctantly, he nodded, tears brimming in his eyes. "Okay, Maya. I'll support you. But promise me you'll come back."

Maya: "I promise, Kabir. Thank you for understanding. I love you."

The Amaranthine Promises: Where love finds its way in the labyrinth of fate, illuminating the path to redemption and renewal. With each page turned, you may find solace in the power of forgiveness and boundless depths of true love.

As they hugged, Kabir couldn't shake the feeling of dread. Deep down, he feared this decision would change everything. And as Maya's departure day approached, his heart grew heavier with each passing moment. Kabir pleaded with Maya to stay, his heart felt heavy with desperation and sorrow. He couldn't bear the thought of losing her, of watching her walk away from everything they had built together. But Maya's mind was made up, her resolve unshakeable as she turned a deaf ear to his pleas. With each word that fell from Maya's lips, Kabir felt his world crumbling around him. He had never imagined that their love could come to such a bitter end, that the woman he had once adored could turn her back on him so callously.

Maya eagerly began packing her belongings, her hands moving swiftly as she carefully selected the items, she would take with her on this new journey. Each item she packed carried with it the promise of a brighter future, a future filled with possibility and opportunity. He watched silently as Maya packed her bags. His heart heavy with the knowledge that their once-strong bond was now fraying at the edges. And as Maya danced out the door, her eyes shining with anticipation, Kabir couldn't help but wonder if their love would be enough to withstand the distance and the challenges that lay ahead. Maya's final decision became clear, a single tear escaped from her eye, glistening like a cruel mockery of the love they had once shared. She walked away, her back turned to him without a second glance. Finally, Maya left, taking a piece of Kabir's heart with her.

It was what felt like a final goodbye, a cold and heartless farewell that left Kabir reeling with pain and disbelief. Maya's

The Amaranthine Promises: Where love finds its way in the labyrinth of fate, illuminating the path to redemption and renewal. With each page turned, you may find solace in the power of forgiveness and boundless depths of true love.

departure felt like disloyalty, a deception of the promises they had made to each other and the dreams they had once held dear. As the days turned into weeks and the weeks into months, Kabir's persistence never waned. He poured his heart and soul into every message, every call, hoping against hope that Maya would respond, that she would remember the love they once shared. But as time stretched on and Maya's silence persisted, Kabir found himself grappling with doubt and uncertainty. Was their love truly as resilient as he believed? Could it weather the storm of Maya's indifference, or was it destined to fade into oblivion like so many others? Kabir couldn't help but wonder how he had ever been so blind to the cruelty that lurked beneath Maya's beautiful exterior.

Looking back in time now, Kabir realizes how foolish he was to push away the very people who cared for him the most, all in the name of a love that ultimately proved fleeting. His tunnel vision had cost him dearly, straining his relationships and isolating him from the support network that could have helped him see the truth sooner. Kabir realizes the toll his singleminded pursuit of Maya took on his friendships. He regrets the moments he missed out on, the memories left unmade, and the bonds that weakened in his absence. But in the throes of love, he couldn't see beyond the narrow scope of his own desires, until it was too late.

Alone once more, Kabir found himself adrift in a sea of uncertainty. He tried to distract himself with work and friends, but the ache of Maya's absence lingered like a ghost, haunting him at every turn. Despite the doubts that crept into his mind, Kabir refused to give up. He clung to the memories

The Amaranthine Promises: Where love finds its way in the labyrinth of fate, illuminating the path to redemption and renewal. With each page turned, you may find solace in the power of forgiveness and boundless depths of true love.

of their time together, the laughter, the joy, the shared dreams. And with each unanswered message, each ignored call, his determination only grew stronger. For Kabir, love was not just a fleeting emotion, but a steadfast commitment, a bond that transcended time and space. And though Maya's silence pierced his heart like a dagger, he remained resolute in his belief that their love would endure, that it would find a way to overcome the barriers that threatened to tear them apart. And so, even as the days stretched into weeks and the weeks into months, Kabir continued to reach out to Maya, holding onto the flicker of hope that burned brightly in his heart. For in the depths of his soul, he knew that true love, the kind of love they shared, was worth fighting for, no matter the odds.

Amidst the flickering glow of a campfire, Kabir and Maya find themselves drawn into a web of revelation and introspection. As the flames dance and crackle, secrets are unveiled, and truths are laid bare, illuminating the hidden depths of their souls and forging an unbreakable bond between them. But destiny had other plans!

The Amaranthine Promises: Where love finds its way in the labyrinth of fate, illuminating the path to redemption and renewal. With each page turned, you may find solace in the power of forgiveness and boundless depths of true love.

Chapter 3
Unveiling the Deception

The love that once bloomed between Kabir and Maya was the envy of all who knew them—a radiant inspiration in a world often dimmed by cynicism and doubt. Their relationship was a testament to the power of love, an idyllic union that seemed destined for eternity. However, beneath the surface of their seemingly perfect romance lurked a shadow—a shadow that would soon eclipse their once bright future. Maya's venture into the unknown began with a single step, but it felt more like a leap into a swirling abyss of uncertainty and excitement. Leaving behind the familiar sights and sounds of her small town, she found herself thrust into the heart of a bustling metropolis, where towering skyscrapers reached for the heavens like giants straining to touch the stars.

The city was a symphony of sights and sounds, a cacophony of chaos and creativity that enveloped Maya like a whirlwind. Everywhere she turned, there were neon lights flashing, cars honking, and people rushing past in a blur of motion and momentum. It was a far cry from the quiet simplicity of her hometown, but Maya was exhilarated by the energy and vitality that pulsed through the city's streets like a heartbeat. As she navigated the complex maze of concrete and glass, Maya felt like a small fish swimming in an ocean of endless possibilities. The skyscrapers soared overhead like

The Amaranthine Promises: Where love finds its way in the labyrinth of fate, illuminating the path to redemption and renewal. With each page turned, you may find solace in the power of forgiveness and boundless depths of true love.

monolithic sentinels guarding the secrets of the city, their reflective surfaces shimmering in the sunlight like beacons of hope and opportunity. With each passing day, Maya's sense of wonder and awe grew stronger, as she explored the city's hidden gems and uncovered its myriad mysteries. From the bustling markets of Chinatown to the tranquil parks nestled amidst the urban jungle, Maya embraced every new experience with open arms, eager to soak in the sights, sounds, and smells of her new surroundings.

But amidst the hustle and bustle of city life, Maya also faced challenges and obstacles that tested her resolve and determination. From navigating the maze-like subway system to finding her way in a sea of unfamiliar faces, Maya learned to rely on her instincts and intuition to guide her through the chaos. Yet despite the trials and tribulations, Maya remained undeterred in her pursuit of her dreams. With each passing day, she grew stronger and more confident, forging new friendships and connections that would shape her journey in ways she never imagined. And as she stood atop a skyscraper, gazing out at the city skyline shimmering in the twilight, Maya felt a sense of peace and fulfilment taking over her like a warm embrace. Maya knew that she had found her place in the world, a shining star in the vast constellation of the city's dreams. As Maya ventured into the unknown, chasing her dreams in a new city, Kabir remained steadfast in his devotion, his love unwavering despite the miles that stretched between them. Little did he know, Maya's heart was beginning to stray, lured by the tantalizing promise of new experiences and forbidden desires.

In her new surroundings, Maya found herself drawn to the company of strangers, their whispered promises of excitement and adventure beckoning her into their midst. Among them was a man whose charm and charisma captivated Maya in ways Kabir never could. Maya's encounter with the enigmatic stranger was like a scene from a romantic movie, unfolding in slow motion against the backdrop of the bustling city streets. A rooftop bar in the city, where the lights of the skyscrapers twinkle in the distance. Maya is sipping on a cocktail, enjoying the cool breeze when a man with a confident aura and a magnetic smile approaches her.

Man: (smiling) "You look like you're lost in thoughts. Mind if I join you and help you find your way?"

Maya: (glancing up, her interest piqued by his confidence) "Not at all. I could use some good company tonight."

Man: (sitting down beside her) "I'm Noah, by the way. And you must be…?"

Maya: (flashing a coy smile) "Maya. Nice to meet you, Noah. So, what brings you to a place like this?"

Noah: (leaning in slightly, his eyes locking onto hers) "I could ask you the same thing, but I'm guessing you're here for the same reason I am— escaping the chaos of the day, seeking something... different."

Maya: (intrigued by his directness) "Different, huh? And what is it you're seeking, exactly?"

Noah: (his voice dropping to a more intimate tone) "Something that makes me feel alive. Someone who isn't afraid to chase after what they want, no matter the cost."

Maya: (her pulse quickens, feeling drawn to his words) "That's a dangerous game, Noah. What if you end up getting more than you bargained for?"

Noah: (smirking) "That's a risk I'm willing to take, especially when the stakes are high. And you, Maya, seem like someone worth taking risks for."

Maya: (biting her lip slightly, the flirtation between them becoming more charged) "You don't even know me."

Noah: (his gaze intense, not breaking eye contact) "Yet, I feel like I do. There's something about you, Maya. You've got this fire inside you, something that's just waiting to be unleashed."

Maya: (feeling the tension build, her guard lowering) "Maybe you're right. Maybe I've been holding back, waiting for someone to light the match."

Noah: (his hand lightly brushing against hers, sending a spark through her) "Then let me be that someone. Life's too short to hold back, don't you think?" His charm was palpable, his smile infectious, and Maya found herself drawn to him like a moth to a flame.

Maya: (her breath catching as she feels the magnetic pull between them) "Maybe you're right, Noah. Maybe now it's time to stop holding back."

The Amaranthine Promises: Where love finds its way in the labyrinth of fate, illuminating the path to redemption and renewal. With each page turned, you may find solace in the power of forgiveness and boundless depths of true love.

Noah: (leaning in closer, his lips inches from hers) "Then what are we waiting for?" Maya: (closing the distance, her voice a whisper as their lips meets) "Nothing at all."

Maya couldn't help but be captivated by his easy-going demeanour and magnetic personality. Maya found herself hanging on his every word, mesmerized by the way he effortlessly commanded attention wherever he went. With each passing day, Maya felt herself falling deeper under his spell, as if she were being swept away by a tide of emotions she couldn't control. His laughter was like music to her ears, his touch sending shivers down her spine, and Maya knew in that instant that she was hopelessly smitten.

Their encounters became more frequent, their conversations more intimate, and Maya found herself opening up to him in ways she never had with Kabir. He listened with rapt attention, his eyes never leaving hers, and Maya felt as though she could tell him anything, confide in him all her hopes and dreams. But amidst the whirlwind romance and newfound passion, Maya couldn't shake the feeling of guilt that gnawed at her conscience. She knew she was betraying Kabir's trust, but she couldn't deny the undeniable connection she felt with this mysterious stranger. And as they shared stolen moments together, lost in each other's embrace, Maya couldn't help but wonder if this was what true love felt like. Was it possible to fall in love with someone new while still holding onto the memories of the past? Or was she simply chasing a fleeting fantasy, a mirage in the desert of her heart? Only time would tell, but for now, Maya allowed herself to bask in the warmth of the stranger's affection, losing herself

The Amaranthine Promises: Where love finds its way in the labyrinth of fate, illuminating the path to redemption and renewal. With each page turned, you may find solace in the power of forgiveness and boundless depths of true love.

in the dizzying whirlwind of passion and desire. And as she leaned in to kiss him, she knew that her life would never be the same again.

Maya's infidelity spiralled out of control, Kabir remained blissfully unaware, his trust in her unshaken by the distance that separated them. As Maya ventured into the bustling city, Kabir remained rooted in their small but enchanting town, a place that seemed to exist in a world of its own. Surrounded by lush greenery, majestic mountains, and clear blue skies, their town was a picture-perfect paradise, a haven of tranquillity amidst the chaos of the outside world.

Every corner of their town was filled with natural wonders, from vibrant rainbows arcing across the sky after a refreshing rain shower to meadows carpeted with pink flowers that bloomed in abundance. It was a place where time seemed to stand still, where the beauty of nature unfolded in all its splendour, captivating the hearts of all who called it home. Despite the physical distance between them, Kabir's trust in Maya remained unshakeable, unwavering in the face of temptation and uncertainty. He held onto the memories of their shared moments, cherishing each precious memory like a priceless treasure that no amount of time or distance could diminish.

Even as Maya embarked on her own journey of self-discovery in the big city, Kabir remained steadfast in his devotion, his love for her transcending the boundaries of time and space. He found solace in the beauty of their town, drawing strength from its serene landscapes and the unwavering support of his friends and family. And though he longed for Maya's presence beside him, Kabir took comfort in the knowledge that their love was as enduring as the mountains that surrounded them, as constant as the ever-changing seasons. For in their small but beautiful town, amidst the wonders of nature and the warmth of their community, Kabir knew that their love would endure, unyielding and eternal.

Soon whispers of Maya's double life began to circulate, they gradually reached Kabir's ears, casting a shadow of doubt and uncertainty over their once-idyllic relationship. At first, it was just a faint murmur, a passing rumour that seemed too far-fetched to be true. But as more details emerged and the evidence began to pile up, Kabir could no longer ignore the truth that lay before him. A dimly lit café where Kabir and his colony friends, Viv and Maddy are seated around a small table. The atmosphere is tense, as Viv and Maddy exchange worried glances before speaking.

Maddy: "Kabir, there's something we need to talk about, and it's not easy."

Viv: "Yeah, Kabir. We've noticed something about Maya... She's not who you think she is."

Kabir: [Confused and slightly defensive] "What are you all talking about?"

Viv: [Gently] "Look, Kabir, we care about you. But Maya... she's been seen with someone else, and not just casually."

Maddy: "We didn't want to believe it either, but it's true. We've heard things, seen things."

Viv: [Trying to soften the blow] "We're not saying this to hurt you, man. We just want you to know the truth before it's too late."

Maddy: "I know this is hard, but you deserve someone who's all in, not someone living a double life."

Kabir: [Silent, absorbing the information with a mix of shock and anger]

Viv: [Reaching out to Kabir] "Please, Kabir, don't let her take advantage of you. We're here for you."

Friends and acquaintances began to share snippets of information, painting a picture of Maya's life that was vastly different from the one she had portrayed to Kabir. Stories of late-night rendezvous and secret meetings in dimly lit cafes circulated among their social circle, casting Maya in a new light that Kabir struggled to reconcile with the image of the woman he thought he knew. With each revelation, Kabir's heart sank a little lower, his faith in Maya crumbling like a house of cards. He couldn't believe that the woman he loved, the woman he had planned a future with, could be leading such a double life, betraying his trust and deceiving him at every turn.

Yet, as much as he wanted to deny the truth, the evidence was undeniable, and Kabir found himself grappling with a mix of emotions – anger, betrayal, and heartbreak. He couldn't help but wonder how he had been so blind, so naive to the truth that had been hiding in plain sight all along. And as the whispers grew louder and the truth became impossible to ignore, Kabir was forced to confront the harsh reality of Maya's deception, a reality that shattered the illusion of their

The Amaranthine Promises: Where love finds its way in the labyrinth of fate, illuminating the path to redemption and renewal. With each page turned, you may find solace in the power of forgiveness and boundless depths of true love.

perfect love and left him reeling with pain and confusion. Driven by a mix of disbelief and heartbreak, Kabir made the impulsive decision to confront Maya in person, hoping to salvage their relationship and restore the trust that had been shattered by her betrayal. As Kabir grappled with the rumors and whispers surrounding Maya's double life, he found himself consumed by a relentless storm of emotions. Doubt gnawed at his insides, a relentless voice in the back of his mind urging him to seek the truth, no matter the cost.

In the quiet solitude of his room, bathed in the soft glow of lamplight, Kabir wrestled with his inner turmoil. He paced the floorboards, his footsteps echoing in the stillness of the night, as he weighed his options and contemplated his next move. With each passing moment, the need to confront Maya grew stronger, a relentless tug at his heart that refused to be ignored. He knew that he couldn't continue living in limbo, suspended between doubt and certainty, forever haunted by the spectre of Maya's betrayal. And so, with a sense of grim determination, Kabir made a decision. He would confront Maya face-to-face, demand answers to the questions that had been plaguing him and lay bare the truth that had been hidden in the shadows for far too long.

The decision weighed heavily on his mind as he prepared for his journey, packing his bags with a sense of urgency that belied the gravity of the situation. Each item he placed in his suitcase was a silent testament to the turmoil raging within him, a physical manifestation of his inner struggle. As he stood on the threshold of his departure, ready to embark on a journey that would change the course of his life forever, Kabir

The Amaranthine Promises: Where love finds its way in the labyrinth of fate, illuminating the path to redemption and renewal. With each page turned, you may find solace in the power of forgiveness and boundless depths of true love.

couldn't help but feel a sense of trepidation mingled with a flicker of hope. He knew that the road ahead would be fraught with uncertainty, but he was determined to face whatever lay ahead with courage and resolve. With one final glance back at the life he was leaving behind, Kabir took a deep breath and stepped forward into the unknown, his heart heavy with the burden of the truth that awaited him in Maya's city.

As Kabir stepped out of the cab and gazed up at Maya's small apartment building, a twinge of sadness engulfed him. Gone were the sprawling landscapes and picturesque views of their small town, replaced instead by the hustle and bustle of city life and the towering skyscrapers that loomed overhead. Maya's apartment was a far cry from the beautiful home they had once shared in their small town. Where once there had been lush gardens and wide-open spaces, now there were cramped streets and crowded sidewalks. The air was thick with the scent of exhaust fumes and the constant hum of traffic filled the air.

Kabir took a moment to compose himself before climbing the stairs to Maya's apartment. His heart raced with a mix of anxiety and determination as he reached her door. With a deep breath, he knocked softly, his hand trembling slightly as he waited for her to answer. When Maya finally opened the door, her eyes widened in surprise at the sight of Kabir standing there. There was a flicker of uncertainty in her expression, as if she wasn't quite sure what to make of his unexpected visit.

"Kabir, what are you doing here?" she asked, her voice tinged with surprise and a hint of nervousness.

"I needed to see you," Kabir replied, his voice steady despite the turmoil churning inside him. "Can we talk?"

Maya hesitated for a moment before nodding, stepping aside to let him into her apartment. As Kabir crossed the threshold, he couldn't help but feel a sense of sadness at the sight of her small, cluttered living space. It was a far cry from the home they had once shared, a stark reminder of how much their lives had changed. But despite the differences, Kabir was determined to get to the bottom of things. He had come here for answers, and he wasn't going to leave until he had them. With a steely resolve, he followed Maya into her apartment, steeling himself for whatever revelations lay ahead.

As Kabir stepped into Maya's apartment, he couldn't shake the feeling that something was off. There was a tension in the air, a sense of unease that hung heavy in the small space. Maya's attempts to act nonchalant only served to heighten Kabir's suspicions. He could sense that she was hiding something, her eyes darting nervously around the room as she tried to maintain her composure.

"I... I have to go out for a bit," Maya stammered, her voice strained. "Can we talk later?"

Kabir felt a sinking feeling in the pit of his stomach, a gnawing sense of dread that told him something wasn't right. But he nodded, forcing a small smile as he replied, "Sure, we can talk later." As Maya hurriedly gathered her things and made for the door, Kabir's instincts kicked in. He knew he had to find out what Maya was hiding, and he couldn't let her leave without getting some answers. "Wait," he blurted out, reaching out to grab her arm. "I'll walk you to your car."

Maya's eyes widened in surprise, but she didn't protest as Kabir guided her out of the apartment and down the hallway. With each step, Kabir's heart pounded in his chest, his mind racing with possibilities of what he might discover. As they reached the building's entrance, Maya turned to face him, a nervous smile playing on her lips. But before she could say anything, Kabir's gaze drifted past her, his eyes narrowing as he caught sight of a figure lurking in the shadows nearby. Without a second thought, Kabir stepped forward, his instincts screaming at him to confront the mysterious stranger. But as he moved closer, the figure melted away into the darkness, leaving Kabir standing alone in the empty street, his mind reeling with unanswered questions.

His mind was consumed with a mixture of dread and determination. He couldn't shake the feeling that something was seriously wrong, and he needed answers. And so Kabir returned to Maya's apartment later that night, as he approached the door, he could hear muffled voices coming from inside. His heart pounding in his chest, Kabir pushed the door open slowly, revealing a scene that made his blood run cold. There, in the dimly lit apartment, Maya stood locked in a passionate embrace with another man. Kabir's breath caught in his throat as he recognized the familiar figure from earlier, the same man who had been lurking in the shadows outside.

Noah: (smirking, watching Maya closely) "You've got Kabir wrapped around your finger, don't you?"

Maya: (with a knowing smile) "I wouldn't say wrapped around. But I know how to keep him guessing."

Noah: (laughing softly) "Guessing? He's been chasing you for ages. That's not guessing, that's hoping."

Maya: (shrugging nonchalantly) "Hoping, chasing—it's all the same. He's too proud to admit it, but I know exactly how he feels. He just doesn't know what to do with it."

Noah: "So what's the plan now? You've got him on a string, Maya. But... are you really in control?"

Maya: (leaning forward, smirking) "Of course I am. That's the beauty of it, Noah. I make it look effortless, like it's all his choice. He thinks he's in charge, but I've always known how to play the game."

Noah: (pausing, studying her) "So what's the endgame here? You're not just playing him for fun, right?"

Maya: (laughing lightly) "Why does there always have to be an endgame? Sometimes, you just enjoy the ride. And believe me, I've been enjoying this one."

Noah: (with a raised eyebrow) "So, it's just about keeping him hooked?" Maya: (sighing, looking out the window) "It's not that simple. He's complicated, you know? But I know I have him. And when the time's right, I'll make sure he knows it too."

Noah: (leaning in, his voice lower) "You think you've got him? You're playing with fire, Maya. People like him don't stay caught forever."

The Amaranthine Promises: Where love finds its way in the labyrinth of fate, illuminating the path to redemption and renewal. With each page turned, you may find solace in the power of forgiveness and boundless depths of true love.

Maya: (smiling confidently) "I know what I'm doing. Trust me, I can handle Kabir. I always have."

Noah: (shaking his head) "I don't know... you're walking a fine line here."

Maya: (with a mischievous smile) "There's no line, Noah. Not with me. You underestimate me if you think I can't get what I want."

Noah: (pausing, then standing up) "Just make sure you're not playing a game that's going to backfire."

Maya: (her tone light, but her eyes hard) "I never lose, Noah. Not when it really matters."

Anger and betrayal surged through Kabir like a tidal wave, threatening to overwhelm him. He stood frozen in the doorway, unable to tear his eyes away from the scene unfolding before him. Maya's laughter echoed in the air, mingling with the sound of the stranger's voice as they whispered sweet nothings to each other. It was a cruel mockery of the love that Kabir had once believed in, a stark reminder of the lies and deceit that had torn their relationship apart. For a moment, Kabir felt as though the world had come crashing down around him. But then, with a steely resolve, he squared his shoulders and forced himself to take a step forward.

There would be no turning back now. He had seen the truth with his own eyes, and he knew that he could never go back to the way things were before. Maya had betrayed him in the cruellest of ways, her actions a stark reminder of the fragility of trust and the depths of human depravity. As Maya's betrayal crashed down upon him, Kabir felt his heart shatter into a million irreparable pieces, the pain of her deception carving deep wounds in his soul. Maya ceased to be the woman he loved and became something else entirely—a monster masquerading as an angel, her beauty a facade for the darkness that lurked within. With tears streaming down his face, Kabir turned away without uttering a word, his faith in love shattered beyond repair. And as he stumbled into the night, the echoes of Maya's laughter ringing in his ears, he vowed to never again trust in the illusion of love— for in the end, it was nothing more than a cruel trick, a lie woven from the threads of deceit and betrayal.

But destiny had other plans in store for Kabir, plans that would test his resolve and push him to the brink of despair. As he wandered the streets in a daze, lost in the darkness of his own grief, dealing with the shock and devastation of discovering Maya's betrayal, his mind was clouded with a tumultuous whirlwind of emotions. Maya's betrayal had pierced his heart like a dagger. Fate intervened in the form of a speeding car hurtling towards him with deadly intent. Kabir failed to notice the oncoming car until it was too late. The screech of tires and the blinding glare of headlights filled his senses, and in the blink of an eye, his world was plunged into darkness.

The impact was sudden and brutal, sending Kabir hurtling through the air before crashing to the unforgiving pavement below. It was a moment of reckoning, Kabir's world came crashing down around him, shattering of glass drowning out the echoes of his shattered heart. Pain ripped through his body like a wildfire, each heartbeat a searing reminder of the

The Amaranthine Promises: Where love finds its way in the labyrinth of fate, illuminating the path to redemption and renewal. With each page turned, you may find solace in the power of forgiveness and boundless depths of true love.

agony he was enduring. In the moments that followed, Kabir's world faded into a hazy blur of sirens and flashing lights as paramedics rushed to his side.

The sound of their voices was distant and indistinct, lost amidst the cacophony of his own thoughts and fears. As he lay broken and bleeding on the unforgiving asphalt, Kabir's mind swirled with fragments of memory and flashes of pain- a thought of Maya, of the woman who had betrayed him in the cruellest of ways, her laughter still echoing in his ears as darkness closed in around him.

But amidst the pain and confusion, one thing became painfully clear – nothing would ever be the same again. But even as he teetered on the brink of oblivion, As Kabir lay battered and broken on the pavement, his consciousness flickering like a dying flame, a stranger amongst the paramedics emerged from the chaos of the night. His face a blur of concern and compassion as he reached out to Kabir in his hour of need. With a sense of urgency and determination, the stranger rushed to Kabir's side, his hands steady and his movements purposeful. With deft precision, the stranger assessed Kabir's injuries, his trained eyes scanning for signs of life amidst the wreckage of the accident. With each passing moment, the stranger's actions grew more urgent, his focus unwavering as he worked tirelessly to stabilize Kabir's condition.

In those crucial moments, the stranger's skill and determination proved to be Kabir's salvation, his quick thinking and unwavering resolve saving him from the jaws of death. With each passing second, the stranger's efforts became a lifeline, pulling Kabir back from the edge and giving him a

The Amaranthine Promises: Where love finds its way in the labyrinth of fate, illuminating the path to redemption and renewal. With each page turned, you may find solace in the power of forgiveness and boundless depths of true love.

second chance at life. And as the chaos of the night began to fade into the background, Kabir found himself overwhelmed with gratitude for the stranger who had come to his rescue. In that fleeting moment of connection, he knew that he owed his life to the kindness and compassion of a stranger – a debt he could never hope to repay. With a gentle touch and a reassuring voice, the stranger pulled Kabir back from the brink, offering him a lifeline in his darkest hour.

Soon Kabir drifted into unconsciousness, his mind awash with pain and regret, a single question burned in his soul—how could he ever find peace in a world torn apart by betrayal and deceit? And yet, as he slipped into the embrace of oblivion, a glimmer of hope flickered in the darkness—a hope that someday, somehow, he would find the strength to rise again from the ashes of his shattered dreams.

As the facade of Maya's perfect image begins to crumble, Kabir is forced to confront the harsh reality of deception and betrayal. With each layer of illusion stripped away, they grapple with the painful realization that the object of their affection may not be who they seem, leading them down a path of doubt and uncertainty.

The Amaranthine Promises: Where love finds its way in the labyrinth of fate, illuminating the path to redemption and renewal. With each page turned, you may find solace in the power of forgiveness and boundless depths of true love.

Chapter 4
Shadows of Solitude

As Kabir lay in his hospital bed, his mind drifted back to the carefree days of college, where he and Maya had shared countless moments of laughter and joy.

Kabir [Hypnagogic Hallucination]: "Hey Maya, I want to share something, Last night, I had a dream about us. We were lying on the floor, your head resting gently on my outstretched arm, our faces close, looking into each other's eyes. We were talking, well mostly you were talking, your voice filling the space between us, while I listened, completely absorbed in every word.

We were smiling a lot, lost in our own world, when it suddenly hit me— wait, we're actually lying on the floor. Just as I was processing this, a small girl casually walked past us like it was the most normal thing ever. I pointed this out to you, expecting some kind of reaction, but you just smiled, shrugged, and asked, "Do you care?" It was like you knew how ridiculous the whole thing was, but that just made it more perfect.

It felt a bit strange since I hadn't dreamt of us in what seems like a decade. But when I woke up, I couldn't help but feel a quiet sense of warmth, like the dream had left behind a subtle, lasting contentment."

The Amaranthine Promises: Where love finds its way in the labyrinth of fate, illuminating the path to redemption and renewal. With each page turned, you may find solace in the power of forgiveness and boundless depths of true love.

But in a wink, those memories felt like distant echoes, haunting reminders of a happiness that had slipped through his fingers. Instead of laughter, Kabir's thoughts were consumed by pain – both physical and emotional. The accident had left him battered and broken, his body aching with every movement. But it was the ache in his heart that hurt the most, the deep sense of loss and betrayal that gnawed at him from within. As he lay there, alone in the dimly lit hospital room, Kabir couldn't shake the feeling of emptiness that enveloped him. Maya's absence weighed heavily on his mind, a constant reminder of the love he had lost and the betrayal he had endured.

The days blurred together in a haze of grief and confusion for Kabir. With Maya gone, his world felt empty and devoid of purpose. Every corner of their once-shared space seemed to echo with her absence, a painful reminder of all that he had lost. His mind drifted back to the fun filled days of college. Despite the pain and heartache of the present, Kabir couldn't help but smile as he recalled the antics and adventures they had experienced together.

One particular memory stood out in Kabir's mind, a hilarious mishap during a college prank gone wrong. He and Maya had teamed up to pull off the ultimate practical joke on their unsuspecting classmates, only to find themselves caught in the crossfire of their own scheme. As Kabir recounted the details of their escapade, he couldn't help but laugh at the sheer absurdity of the situation. From dodging security guards to narrowly escaping capture, the memory was a testament to

The Amaranthine Promises: Where love finds its way in the labyrinth of fate, illuminating the path to redemption and renewal. With each page turned, you may find solace in the power of forgiveness and boundless depths of true love.

the bond he and Maya shared – a bond forged in laughter and mischief.

Unable to escape the memories that haunted him at every turn, Kabir found himself sinking deeper into despair with each passing day. He withdrew from his friends, his work, and the world around him, retreating into a cocoon of solitude where his pain could consume him without interruption. Maya's departure pressed down on him like a leaden blanket, suffocating him with its oppressive presence. He tried to fill the void with distractions - alcohol, partying, meaningless flings - but nothing could dull the ache of her absence.

Nights stretched into days, and days into weeks, but still, Kabir remained trapped in the grip of his grief. He wandered aimlessly through the streets, his footsteps echoing in the empty silence of the night, searching for solace in the darkness. Gone were the days of laughter and mischief, replaced now by the cold reality of loneliness and regret. And as he stared up at the ceiling, listening to the steady rhythm of his own breathing, Kabir couldn't help but wonder if he would ever find peace again.

In every corner of the town, Maya's presence seemed to linger like a ghost, haunting Kabir's every step. Whether he was grabbing a coffee at their favourite cafe, strolling through the bustling streets, or taking a solitary walk in the park, memories of Maya followed him like shadows. But it was the mountain that held the most potent memories for Kabir. It was their sanctuary, their refuge from the chaos of the world below. They had spent countless hours there, riding their bikes along winding trails, breathing in the crisp mountain air,

The Amaranthine Promises: Where love finds its way in the labyrinth of fate, illuminating the path to redemption and renewal. With each page turned, you may find solace in the power of forgiveness and boundless depths of true love.

and marvelling at the breath-taking views. Now, Kabir found himself returning to the mountain alone, seeking solace in the familiar surroundings that had once been filled with laughter and love. He would sit on their favourite spot, overlooking the valley below, and close his eyes, trying to conjure up the echoes of Maya's laughter. But the mountain offered no solace, no comfort, only a stark reminder of all that he had lost. And as he sat there, surrounded by the beauty of nature, Kabir couldn't help but feel the weight of Maya's absence pressing down on him like a heavy stone.

As Kabir sat alone on the mountain, his mind wandered back to a painful memory that seemed to taunt him relentlessly. It was Valentine's Day, and Maya had expressed her desire for a crystal teddy bear she had seen displayed on a crystal seesaw in a shop window. Filled with love and eager to fulfill Maya's wish, Kabir had rushed to the store, only to find that the crystal teddy bear was far beyond his budget. Despite his efforts to find a more affordable alternative, he couldn't shake the feeling of disappointment that he couldn't give Maya what she wanted. Now, as he replayed the scene in his mind, Kabir couldn't help but blame himself for not being able to provide for Maya's desires. He felt like he had failed her, like he wasn't enough to make her happy. His inadequacy hung heavy on his shoulders, crushing him with each passing moment.

And as he gazed out at the breath-taking vista before him, Kabir couldn't help but feel a cramp of regret for all the times he had fallen short in Maya's eyes. It was a wound that seemed to deepen with each passing day, a reminder of his own perceived shortcomings in the eyes of the woman he loved. It was in these moments of quiet reflection that Kabir's thoughts turned inward, grappling with the painful truth of his own shortcomings. He berated himself for not being enough, for failing to keep Maya's love alive, for letting her slip through his fingers like grains of sand. In the aftermath of the devastating breakup, Kabir found himself sinking deeper and deeper into a pit of despair, his once vibrant spirit dulled by heartache and betrayal. But in the darkness, there was one shining beacon of light that refused to be extinguished, his younger brother.

From the moment Kabir's world came crashing down around him, his younger brother stood by his side unwaveringly, a pillar of strength and support in his darkest hour. With a quiet determination and boundless compassion, he refused to let his brother succumb to the suffocating grip of depression, his love for Kabir burning bright even in the bleakest of times.

Karan, Kabir's younger brother, a tall and fair young man with striking hazel eyes. Alongside his handsome appearance, Karan possessed a strength of character and a deep sensitivity that set him apart. From a young age, he had always been fiercely protective of Kabir, standing by his side through thick and thin. With a heart as big as his stature, Karan was known for his unwavering loyalty and his ability to empathize with others. He had a knack for seeing past the surface and understanding the emotions that lay beneath, making him a trusted confidant and a reliable source of support for Kabir.

As Kabir navigated the ups and downs of life, Karan was always there, offering words of wisdom and a shoulder to lean on. Whether it was a heartbreak or a triumph, Karan stood by his brother's side, ready to offer a listening ear and a comforting presence. Despite their occasional differences, Karan and Kabir shared a bond that ran deep, rooted in love, respect, and an unbreakable brotherhood. Every day, without fail, Karan would wait patiently for Kabir to come home from work, a warm meal and a sympathetic ear always at the ready. He would listen as Kabir poured out his heart, his own pain and sorrow echoing in the depths of his eyes, yet never once wavering in his resolve to be there for his elder brother. But it wasn't just emotional support that Karan provided. It was the little things, the small acts of kindness and selflessness that spoke volumes more than words ever could. He would make sure Kabir ate three square meals a day, even if it meant coaxing him out of bed and sitting with him until he finished every last bite. He would accompany Kabir on long walks through the park, a silent presence at his side as they wandered aimlessly, lost in their own thoughts.

One day, Kabir sitting hunched over on the edge of his bed, his face buried in his hands,

Kabir: [voice barely above a whisper] "I can't believe she did this, Karan. How could she? How did I not see it? I feel like such an idiot."

Karan: [Quietly walks in, his expression hardening as he sees his brother's broken form. He sits beside Kabir, his voice steady but soft] "You weren't an idiot, Kabir. You were in love. You trusted her... you gave her everything you had."

Kabir: [Shaking his head violently, the pain and disbelief in his voice growing stronger] "But I was blind, Karan. Blind! Everyone saw it but me. She was slipping away right in front of me, and I... I just let it happen. She was lying to my face, and I let her."

Karan: [His eyes darken, anger swelling in his chest as he places a hand on Kabir's back] "She manipulated you. You loved her, and she took advantage of that. You can't blame yourself for trusting someone you thought was your future."

Kabir: [tears stream down his face, but he doesn't bother to wipe them away. His voice cracks as he speaks] "I gave her everything, Karan. My time, my energy... I distanced myself from everyone—my friends, my family. I thought if I loved her enough, I could make it work. But... I wasn't enough. I was never enough for her."

Karan: [Firmly grips Kabir's shoulders, his voice filled with a mixture of sadness and protectiveness] "That's not true. You were always enough. She's the one who wasn't enough. You gave her more than she deserved, and she didn't even have the decency to appreciate it. She's the one who's broken, Kabir, not you."

Kabir: [His voice breaks as he looks at Karan, eyes full of desperation] "Then why does it feel like I'm the one falling apart? Why does it hurt so much? I loved her, Karan. I thought... I thought she was it. My forever."

Karan: [Tears well up in his own eyes as he watches his brother unravel, but he holds his voice steady, refusing to show his own pain] "Because you loved her deeply, Kabir. And that's not something to be ashamed of. You loved her with your whole heart, and she threw it away. But one day, this pain will fade. It will. And when it does, you'll see that you're better off without her. You'll find someone who deserves you, who would never throw away the love you give."

Kabir: [His voice is barely audible, a broken whisper] "I don't know if I can believe that anymore."

Karan: [Pulling Kabir into a hug, his voice choked with emotion as he holds his brother tight] "You don't have to believe it right now. That's okay. But I'll believe it for you. I'll be here, every step of the way, until you can see it for yourself. I won't let you go through this alone."

Kabir: [His sobs grow heavier as he clings to Karan, his heartbreak finally breaking through the numbness he's been feeling] "I don't know what to do, Karan. I don't know how to move forward."

Karan: [Stroking Kabir's back, his own voice shaking with the pain of seeing his brother like this] "One step at a time, bro. We'll get through this. Together. You have me, and I'm not going anywhere. Ever. You hear me? We'll figure this out."

Kabir: [Through the tears, his voice filled with helplessness] "It hurts so much... I don't think it'll ever stop."

Karan: [Holding Kabir even tighter, whispering softly but fiercely] "It will. I promise. It won't feel like this forever. But until it does, I'll carry some of that hurt with you. You're not alone, Kabir. You'll never be alone."

When the nights grew long and the loneliness threatened to consume Kabir whole, his younger brother would sit with him in the darkness. It was in the stillness of the night when Kabir's world was shrouded in darkness and silence. Kabir would often find himself engulfed in a torrent of emotions. It was during these moments of vulnerability that he would cry out loud, his anguish echoing through the empty corridors of their home. Karan, ever vigilant, would rush to his brother's side, drawn by the rawness of Kabir's pain. Without hesitation, he would envelop Kabir in a tight embrace, holding him close as tears streamed down their faces. In that shared moment of vulnerability, the brothers found solace in each other's arms, their silent embrace speaking volumes of the unbreakable bond between them. And as the night wore on, Karan remained by Kabir's side, a steadfast presence in the midst of his brother's storm. He would hold Kabir as he cried, his arms a safe haven in the storm, his love a lifeline in the tumultuous sea of grief, a comforting presence in the silence, his unwavering love a beacon of hope in the vast expanse of despair.

But perhaps most importantly, Karan never gave up on him, never lost faith in his ability to rise above the pain and find his way back to the light. With every word of encouragement, every gesture of kindness, he reminded Kabir that he was not alone, that no matter how dark the night may seem, there was always a glimmer of hope on the horizon. And so, as the days turned into weeks and the weeks turned into months, Karan remained by his side, a steadfast companion on the journey through the valley of shadows. And though the road ahead may have been long and arduous, they walked it together, hand in hand, heart to heart, brothers bound by a love that would never falter, a love that would carry them through even the darkest of nights.

The Amaranthine Promises: Where love finds its way in the labyrinth of fate, illuminating the path to redemption and renewal. With each page turned, you may find solace in the power of forgiveness and boundless depths of true love.

As Kabir grappled with the fallout of his breakup with Maya, he found himself facing not only the crushing heaviness of heartache but also the sting of betrayal from those he once considered his closest friends, his college gang. Unaware of the complexities of the situation and fuelled by hearsay and half-truths, they quickly rallied around Maya, casting Kabir as the villain in their narrative of the breakup. With each passing day, Kabir felt the walls closing in around him, the once-familiar faces of his friends now twisted with suspicion and distrust. They whispered behind his back, their words like daggers in his heart, painting him as the heartless antagonist in Maya's tragic tale of love gone awry. And as the accusations mounted and the rumours spread like wildfire, Kabir found himself ostracized and isolated, his cries for understanding falling on deaf ears.

Despite their distrust pressing down on him, Kabir couldn't bring himself to confront his friends. The hurt ran too deep, the wounds too fresh to bear. Instead, he watched from a distance, his heart heavy with sadness at the sight of his once tight-knit group fractured by lies and deceit. It was a bitter pill to swallow, knowing that the bonds of friendship he cherished had been shattered beyond repair. And as he stood alone amidst the wreckage of his former life, Kabir couldn't help but wonder if the truth would ever come to light, or if he would forever be branded as the villain in Maya's twisted tale.

But perhaps what hurt the most was the swiftness with which Maya's family turned their backs on him, their loyalty to Maya eclipsing their loyalty to him. As rumours spread like wildfire, Kabir found himself cast in the role of the villain, his

The Amaranthine Promises: Where love finds its way in the labyrinth of fate, illuminating the path to redemption and renewal. With each page turned, you may find solace in the power of forgiveness and boundless depths of true love.

once beloved family friends turning their backs on him without a second thought. They hurled accusations and insults with reckless abandon, their judgment clouded by their unreasoning allegiance to Maya and their desire to see her vindicated at any cost. Blinded by Maya's carefully crafted deception, they assembled around her, offering their unwavering support without bothering to seek the truth. Each accusatory glance, each whispered conversation served as a painful reminder of the betrayal he endured. And as Kabir stood before them, his heart heavy with sorrow and disbelief, he realized that he was truly alone, abandoned by those he once held dear.

It was a rainy day, the kind of downpour that made everything seem quieter and more reflective. Kabir was sitting on the back of Maddy's bike, clinging onto him as they weaved through the slick, water-covered roads. The city had that familiar, wet smell, and the misty air blurred the streetlights, casting a soft glow over everything. The two friends had been riding around for a while, trying to catch up on life.

The rain picked up, making it harder to see, and Maddy cursed under his breath. He pulled over beneath a small roadside shelter, shaking the water off his jacket.

"Man, my phone's soaked," Maddy said, fishing it out of his pocket. He wiped it on his sleeve and then handed it to Kabir. "Hey, can you toss this in your bag for me? I don't want it getting any wetter."

Kabir, still lost in his own thoughts, absentmindedly took the phone. His heart had been heavy for weeks, weighed down by thoughts of Maya and the betrayal that lingered between them like an unshakable shadow.

As Kabir unzipped his bag to store Maddy's phone, it buzzed in his hand. A message notification popped up on the screen. Kabir glanced at it, intending to ignore it, but his breath caught in his throat when he saw the name.

"Maya..."

His eyes instinctively darted to the message preview. It was short, but it spoke volumes:

"Hope you're okay. We should meet soon."

Kabir's heart pounded in his chest. What the hell? He tried to steady his breathing, but the words on the screen felt like knives. This couldn't be happening—Maddy? Of all people?

The rain around them felt deafening, each drop pounding like a drum, amplifying the silence between the two friends. Kabir swallowed hard, unsure of how to react. His mind raced with questions. Why was Maya messaging Maddy? How long had this been going on?

Kabir's grip tightened around Maddy's phone as he slowly lowered it, his pulse quickening, his heart aching.

"Everything alright?" Maddy asked, oblivious to Kabir's internal turmoil, adjusting his helmet as he prepared to get back on the road.

Kabir forced a smile, but it felt hollow, fake. "Yeah, just putting your phone away," he said, his voice strained. His hands were trembling as he stuffed the phone into his bag, his mind reeling with disbelief. He didn't know whether to confront Maddy right then and there or wait for a better time. The rain pounded harder, echoing the storm raging in Kabir's chest.

For the rest of the ride, Kabir sat quietly, the world outside a blur as they drove through the downpour. Every raindrop seemed to amplify the betrayal. Maya, the girl he had loved so deeply, was now messaging his friend—his brother. Maddy, who had been by his side through so much, was talking to her behind his back.

When they finally stopped, Kabir couldn't hold it in anymore. He got off the bike, his clothes drenched and his heart heavier than ever.

"Maddy," Kabir said, his voice low, barely audible over the sound of rain hitting the pavement.

Maddy looked over, a questioning glance in his eyes. "What's up?"

Kabir's throat felt tight as he wrestled with the words. "Are you... talking to Maya?"

Maddy's face tensed, a flash of surprise crossing his features before he quickly masked it. "What do you mean?"

"I saw the message," Kabir said quietly, his voice cracking. "She texted you. Why?"

Maddy sighed, looking away, avoiding eye contact. "It's nothing, man. She was just checking in... you know, after everything. It's no big deal."

It had been a while since Kabir had laughed freely. His friends, Maddy, Viv, and his younger brother, Karan, couldn't bear to see him so withdrawn, consumed by his grief. Something had to be done, Kabir needed to break free from the chains of his own thoughts, even if just for one night.

So, they came up with a plan. A boys' night out, but without actually leaving the house.

The evening started off at Kabir's apartment, where Maddy, Viv, and Karan arrived, armed with snacks and soft drinks, eager to lift their friend's spirits. The apartment, once filled with Kabir's laughter and endless energy, now felt eerily quiet. But tonight, that was going to change. They were here to revive it.

Maddy: (throwing a bag of chips on the coffee table) "Alright, no more moping around, Kabir. We're gonna make this night legendary."

Viv: (grinning) "Yeah, none of that brooding stuff. We're gonna make you laugh tonight, one way or another."

Karan: (already setting up the board games) "Let's start with something simple. You can't get too sad if you're winning at Monopoly, right?"

Kabir forced a small smile, grateful for their persistence, though a part of him felt detached. They pushed him, just like they always had, but the emptiness he felt inside never seemed to lift.

They ate, laughed, and as the evening grew older, the music came on. One by one, each friend played their favourite songs—songs that had been the soundtrack to their many late-night hangouts, songs that once filled the air with energy and life.

Maddy: (cranking up an old classic rock song) "This one's for the 'good old days.' You remember this, Kabir?"

Kabir nodded absently. He did remember, but everything felt distant. The fun he used to have was now just a shadow. But the music, though, the music helped. It pulled him into the present, at least for a little while.

Then came the board games, an attempt to spark something—anything. Cards, dice, and jokes flying across the room. And for a moment, just a moment, Kabir felt the tug of nostalgia, of old times when life had been simpler, and their biggest problem was who'd get the last slice of pizza.

But it wasn't enough. Not yet.

Viv: (after a few hours) "Alright, guys, I have an idea. Let's take this up a notch."

Kabir looked at them, a little confused.

Karan: (with a mischievous grin) "We're going up on the roof."

Kabir raised an eyebrow, half-expecting something ridiculous.

Maddy: (nodding dramatically) "But we do it in style. Blankets, like superheroes. We'll run around the roof under the moonlight. You with me, bro?"

Kabir couldn't help but chuckle, despite himself. There was something absurdly comforting about how ridiculous their plan sounded.

The four of them snuck up to the roof, blankets wrapped around them like capes. They were a motley crew of grown men pretending to be children again, racing across the roof, howling with laughter as the cool night air whipped past them.

Suddenly, from one of the neighbouring houses, a light flicked on. Someone had seen them. They froze in their tracks, watching as a figure peered through the window.

Karan: (giggling) "Do you think they think we're ghosts?"

Maddy: (whispering) "Of course they do. Look at us—blankets flying in the moonlight like we're some kind of haunted spirits."

Viv: (laughing hysterically) "Who needs a Halloween costume when we've got this?"

The evening had been full of laughter, good times, and a ridiculous rooftop adventure that had temporarily lifted Kabir's spirits. But despite the fun, Kabir's heart never fully let go of the wound it carried. He sat quietly now, surrounded by his friends—Viv, Karan, and Maddy. The glow of the evening had faded, and the inevitable conversation hung in the air.

Maddy, who had been unusually quiet for the past hour, could feel the tension in Kabir. It wasn't that Kabir was openly angry, it was the silence that spoke volumes. Kabir had known about Maddy's secret for some time now. He knew Maddy had been in contact with Maya. Kabir wasn't blind to the way

Maddy acted when her name came up, or the subtle phone calls he'd made when Kabir wasn't around. But Kabir had chosen to stay silent, waiting for Maddy to come to him on his own terms.

Now, after all the laughter and distractions, Maddy couldn't escape it anymore. He knew he couldn't hide the truth any longer.

Maddy leaned forward on the couch, his voice low, as he broke the silence.

Maddy: (tentatively) "Kabir... there's something I need to tell you."

Kabir, though he had been expecting this moment, gave Maddy his full attention. His expression was neutral, but his eyes betrayed a faint sorrow—a mix of resignation and patience.

Kabir: (calmly) "I already know, Maddy."

Maddy's breath caught in his throat, his heart pounding. He stared at Kabir, a bit surprised but also relieved that the truth had come out without any need for confrontation.

Maddy: "You knew?"

Kabir nodded slowly, his gaze steady but soft. He had known for weeks, but he hadn't said anything. Part of him wanted to believe Maddy would realize his mistake on his own.

Kabir: (quietly) "Yeah. I've seen the way you've been acting. I know about the calls, about the texts... I knew you were talking to her."

The Amaranthine Promises: Where love finds its way in the labyrinth of fate, illuminating the path to redemption and renewal. With each page turned, you may find solace in the power of forgiveness and boundless depths of true love.

Maddy felt a mass drop in his chest. He opened his mouth to speak, but the words seemed to catch in his throat. He had known Kabir was aware, but hearing him say it aloud made everything real. The guilt was unbearable now.

Maddy: (softly) "I'm sorry, Kabir. I... I don't know why I kept in touch with her. I told myself I was trying to help her, but deep down, I knew I was just making it worse. I should've stopped. I should've respected what happened between you two."

Kabir leaned back on the couch, his arms crossed, but his posture wasn't as rigid as before. He wasn't angry, but the hurt was there, hidden behind his calm demeanour.

Kabir: (quietly) "I don't know why you did it either, Maddy. You were my best friend. I trusted you, and... you kept talking to her after everything that happened. I never asked you to choose sides, but I thought you'd stand by me. I thought you'd understand."

Maddy's face was filled with regret. His eyes met Kabir's, and he could see the pain there, even if Kabir wasn't fully expressing it.

Maddy: (earnestly) "I wasn't choosing sides, Kabir. I was just... I don't know. I guess I was caught up in wanting to believe she could change, that maybe she didn't mean to hurt you like that. But I see now that I was wrong. I should've been there for you, not for her."

Kabir remained quiet for a moment, absorbing Maddy's words. The silence between them was thick, but this wasn't a fight—it was a moment of clarity. Kabir had known Maddy was trying to justify his actions to himself, but now Maddy was finally being honest. That honesty, though painful, was what Kabir had needed.

Kabir: (after a pause) "I get it. You were trying to help, but it was misguided. But it hurt, Maddy. It hurt a lot."

Maddy's eyes were sincere as he reached out slightly, not quite touching Kabir but hoping his words would be enough to bridge the gap between them.

Maddy: (softly) "I can't take it back, Kabir. But I'm sorry for not being there when you needed me. I should've supported you fully, no matter what. I don't want to lose you as a friend over this."

Kabir sat still for a moment, the weight of everything they'd been through settling in his chest. He had been hurt, yes, but he could see the genuine regret in Maddy's eyes. He had been waiting for this moment, for Maddy to admit his mistake, and now that it was happening, Kabir didn't feel the anger he thought he would. Instead, there was a sense of relief.

Kabir: (sighing) "It's not easy, Maddy. What you did wasn't right. But I'm glad you're being real with me now. I think that's all I needed—honesty."

Maddy smiled, a little shakily, but the load on his shoulders seemed to lift. He had hoped for Kabir's forgiveness, but he had never expected it to come so simply, so genuinely.

Maddy: (sincerely) "I'm really sorry, Kabir. I'll make it right, I swear. Just... give me the chance to prove it."

Kabir stood up, moving toward Maddy. Without saying another word, he pulled him into a hug. The embrace wasn't dramatic, but it was filled with the understanding that only old friends could share—years of friendship, mistakes, and forgiveness wrapped in one.

Kabir: (softly) "You don't need to prove anything. Just be here for me, man. That's all I need." Maddy hugged him back, the relief submerged him.

Maddy: "I'm here. Always."

As they pulled apart, both of them knew the road ahead wouldn't be easy. Kabir's pain was still there, and Maddy's mistake wouldn't be forgotten overnight. But tonight, there was hope—a glimmer of it—and that was enough for them both.

The laughter of their earlier games still echoed in the background, but now, it felt a little more genuine, a little more heartfelt.

The next day, rumours spread like wildfire across the neighbourhood. "The haunted house on the block"—that's what everyone was calling it. People were whispering about strange sightings in the night, the 'ghosts' running across the roof.

Kabir and his friends, however, had the best laugh about it.

Kabir: (holding his stomach from laughing) "I can't believe they actually thought we were ghosts!"

Maddy: (tears of laughter in his eyes) "We really are something else, aren't we?"

The Amaranthine Promises: Where love finds its way in the labyrinth of fate, illuminating the path to redemption and renewal. With each page turned, you may find solace in the power of forgiveness and boundless depths of true love.

For the first time in weeks, Kabir felt something resembling happiness— true, unfiltered joy. His friends had brought him back to life, if only for a moment.

But as the laughter died down and the night passed, Kabir returned to his solitude. He sat alone in his apartment again, staring out the window as the sun rose. All his thoughts returned, more suffocating than before.

The emptiness began to creep back in, just like it always did. The loneliness settled around him, thick and suffocating. The night had been an escape, but now it felt like a distant memory.

He wanted to believe that maybe, just maybe, he could break free from the chains of his sorrow. But as reality set in, he realized how deeply the darkness had embedded itself within him. The laughter of the night before lingered in his mind, but it felt like an illusion. A fleeting glimpse of something better, now out of reach. He stood up, walked to the window, and gazed out once more, his heart heavy again. The hope that his friends had given him, that night, seemed too fragile to hold onto. It was back to the quiet, back to the solitude—back to the familiar emptiness that never truly left.

Haunted by the spectre of Maya's disloyalty, Kabir finds himself ensnared in the suffocating grip of solitude. As Maya's betrayal unfolded, Kabir found himself isolated, his friends swayed by false accusations. Yet, amid this turmoil, his brother Karan stood by him unwaveringly, offering solace and support through the darkest of nights. Together, they weathered the storm of deceit, their bond unbreakable amidst the tumult of betrayal...

The Amaranthine Promises: Where love finds its way in the labyrinth of fate, illuminating the path to redemption and renewal. With each page turned, you may find solace in the power of forgiveness and boundless depths of true love.

Chapter 5
Navigating the Darkness

Kabir's descent into madness was marked by erratic behaviour and a haunting sense of desperation. Driven by a desperate longing to see Maya one last time, Kabir's mind became consumed by a single, all-encompassing obsession. Barefoot and dishevelled, he would wander the streets in a daze, his thoughts consumed by visions of her face. People passing by would cast worried glances in his direction, their whispers a harsh reminder of the reality from which he sought to escape. Some would try to intervene, offering words of comfort or attempting to guide him back home, but Kabir's resolve remained unshaken. His feet carried him ever onward, each step a testament to the depths of his misery. The airport beckoned to him like a siren's call, promising the chance to bridge the chasm that separated him from Maya. But with each failed attempt to board a plane, the reality of his situation would come crashing down upon him with renewed force.

Desperate for solace, Kabir would often find himself slipping out of the house in the dead of night, seeking refuge in the empty streets. But no matter how far he wandered, he could never outrun the pain that followed him like a shadow, a constant reminder of all that he had lost. Despite his efforts to escape, Karan always managed to track him down and bring him back home. With patience and persistence, he would coax

Kabir out of his desolation, offering a comforting presence in the midst of his turmoil. However, when Karan's work took him out of town for a few days, Kabir found himself facing his demons alone. The prospect of being without his brother's support filled him with a sense of dread, leaving him feeling more vulnerable than ever before. During Karan's absence, Kabir's restlessness grew with each passing day. He found himself unable to escape the memories of Maya, her absence a constant ache in his heart. In the stillness of the night, when the world around him was shrouded in darkness, the longing for her became almost unbearable.

As Maya's birthday approached, Kabir couldn't shake the memories of their past celebrations. He vividly remembered the time they spent together, like the year they went camping and ended up stargazing by the fire, or the birthday picnic they had in the park, where Maya laughed uncontrollably as they fed each other cake. These memories played like a movie in Kabir's mind, each scene etched with the joy and love they shared. He recalled the way Maya's eyes sparkled with excitement as she opened his gifts, and the warmth of her hand in his as they walked along the beach at sunset.

But amidst the sweetness of these memories, there was also a pang of sadness. Maya's absence on her birthday felt like a void, a reminder of what was lost. On the Birthday, Kabir found himself ensnared in a relentless tug-of-war with his memories. Each corner of his house seemed to echo with the ghost of their past, a haunting reminder of the love they once shared. Despite his best efforts to bury the pain beneath a facade of indifference, the memories continued to claw their way to the surface, refusing to be silenced. Driven by a desperate longing to see Maya one last time, Kabir made the impulsive decision to leave the confines of his home and seek her out. In the stillness of the night, with the world asleep around him, he embarked on a journey fraught with uncertainty, his heart filled with emotions. With a heavy heart, Kabir made the decision to confront Maya one last time, to seek closure in the face of their fractured relationship. The thought of seeing her again filled him with a strange mix of trepidation and longing, but he knew that he could no longer deny the pull of their shared past.

Kabir found himself walking down their favourite street, the one that always felt like it belonged only to him and Maya. It was late afternoon, and the golden sunlight filtered through the trees, casting long shadows on the cobbled road. Everything was just as it used to be—the familiar cafés, the flower shop where Maya once dragged him to smell roses, and the little bookstand that always had her favourite novels. The air was crisp, filled with the scent of blooming jasmine, and Kabir felt light, carefree, like all the pain he'd been carrying had disappeared.

He looked beside him, and there she was—Maya. Her laughter filled the air, that carefree giggle that always made his heart skip a beat. She was wearing that bright yellow dress she loved so much, the one that always made her stand out. They were talking, though Kabir couldn't quite hear what either of them was saying. It didn't matter. Everything felt right. They were together again, walking in step, just like old times. The

The Amaranthine Promises: Where love finds its way in the labyrinth of fate, illuminating the path to redemption and renewal. With each page turned, you may find solace in the power of forgiveness and boundless depths of true love.

street was alive with people passing by, yet it felt as if they were in their own world.

As they walked, Kabir turned to say something to her, but when he glanced over, his heart froze.

Maya was gone.

He stopped, looking around, bewildered. "Maya?" he called, his voice barely above a whisper. He spun in place, searching for her bright dress in the crowd, but she wasn't there. The street had changed in an instant. What was once full of life now felt desolate. The once-busy road was now eerily empty, the flowers wilting, the sunlight fading to a dull, lifeless grey.

Kabir's chest tightened as panic began to swell. "Where did she go?" He started to walk faster, calling her name louder now. "Maya! Maya, where are you?" His voice echoed off the empty buildings, but no answer came. His heart pounded as his steps quickened, each footfall louder in the hollow silence.

The café chairs were toppled over, the flower stand was bare, and the streets that had once felt so familiar now seemed like a twisted, lonely maze. Kabir could hear his own breathing, shallow and frantic. He spun around again, desperate to find her, to bring back that fleeting moment of happiness. But there was nothing—no one.

The town, their street, everything was empty.

Suddenly, his foot slipped, and he fell hard onto the ground. The impact jolted him, and as he looked around from where he lay, the silence pressed in on him like a vice.

The Amaranthine Promises: Where love finds its way in the labyrinth of fate, illuminating the path to redemption and renewal. With each page turned, you may find solace in the power of forgiveness and boundless depths of true love.

His hands gripped the cold, cracked pavement, but the world around him felt like it was crumbling, fading into nothingness.

"Maya!" His voice cracked with fear, but it was swallowed by the void. She was gone. Truly gone.

And then, just like that, everything went black.

Kabir shot up in bed, gasping for breath. His heart was pounding, his body drenched in cold sweat. The room was dark, the only sound the soft hum of the ceiling fan above him. For a moment, he didn't know where he was. His mind was still trapped in that street, still searching for her.

Reality came crashing down like a tidal wave. The dream, so vivid, so real, had shaken him to his core. The emptiness, the vanishing Maya—it felt like his worst fear had manifested. He buried his face in his hands, trying to shake the image from his mind, but it lingered, a haunting reminder of the woman he had lost.

Kabir sat there in the stillness of the night, feeling the ache deep in his chest. The dream was just a reflection of what had been eating away at him for weeks—the fear that Maya wasn't just gone from his life but erased completely, like she had never been there at all. And worse, he was powerless to stop it.

He stared at the ceiling, his mind racing, his heart heavy with the heft of it all. The dream may have ended, but the fear of losing her forever, of being left alone in the empty streets of his memories, was something he couldn't wake up from.

The Amaranthine Promises: Where love finds its way in the labyrinth of fate, illuminating the path to redemption and renewal. With each page turned, you may find solace in the power of forgiveness and boundless depths of true love.

With a sense of resignation, Kabir rose from his bed and made his way to the door, his footsteps echoing in the empty silence of the house. As Kabir's footsteps echoed softly in the empty hallway, his heart heavy with the burden of his shattered dreams, he found himself drawn inexorably towards the front door, each step a reminder of the burden he carried with him wherever he went. As he reached for the doorknob, a flicker of uncertainty crept into his mind, casting doubt upon his decision. But with a steadying breath, Kabir pushed aside his doubts and stepped out into the night, his heart filled with inquisitiveness of what lay ahead. But as he reached out to grasp the doorknob, his hand trembling with uncertainty, he was suddenly brought to a halt by a sight that stopped him dead in his tracks. His parents, sitting side by side in the dimly lit hallway, their faces etched with sorrow and concern.

In the soft glow of the hallway light, Kabir could see the pain etched into the lines of their faces, the weariness in their eyes a mirror of his own soul. His mother's hands trembled as she clutched a tissue to her chest, tears glistening in the corners of her eyes, while his father sat beside her, his shoulders slumped with the weight of the world. Kabir's parents were deeply worried about his well-being as they watched his erratic behaviour unfold. They could see the toll Maya's departure had taken on him, and despite their efforts to offer support, they felt helpless in the face of his suffering. The clock on the wall ticked softly, marking the passing hours, but sleep had eluded both of them. They sat in silence for a long while, side by side on the old wooden bench in the corner, the quiet of the house almost deafening.

She wiped a tear from the corner of her eye, trying to stifle the sob that threatened to break free. "I don't know what to do anymore," she whispered, her voice breaking. "Our boy… he's not the same. He's drowning in pain, and we can't help him."

Kabir's Father sat with his head bowed, his hands clasped tightly in his lap, his heart heavy. "I know," he finally said, his voice low and filled with sorrow. "I see it too. Every day, he's slipping further away from us… from himself."

She pressed her hand to her chest, as if trying to keep her heart from shattering. "This is supposed to be the best time of his life. He's young, he's supposed to be happy, planning for his future… and instead, look at him. He's barely living."

Kabir's Father's eyes welled up, but he blinked back the tears. He needed to stay strong, but even he felt like he was losing his grip. "We raised him to be strong, to face life head-on. But this… this kind of pain, it's… it's unbearable."

She nodded, her hands trembling as they rested on her lap. "He doesn't talk to us anymore. He barely eats, barely sleeps. Sometimes I wonder if he's even really here when he's sitting right in front of us."

"I feel so helpless," he admitted quietly. "I watch him suffer, and I don't know what to do. I don't know how to fix this."

She wept softly now, unable to hold it in any longer. "We can't take this pain away from him, can we?"

"No," he said, his voice barely a whisper. "Not this time."

She shook her head, her tears falling freely now. "I wish I could take it all away… carry it for him… anything to make him smile again."

He looked at her, his own eyes filled with unshed tears, and reached for her hand. "So do I. But all we can do is be here… hope that one day, he'll find a way back to us."

They sat there in the stillness, holding each other's hands, hearts breaking for their son, for the happiness that had been stolen from him. The hallway, once filled with the sounds of Kabir's laughter and joy, now felt like a hollow echo of the life they used to know.

"We'll get through this," father said, though he wasn't sure if he was trying to convince her or himself.

"He'll get through this." She nodded, but the doubt lingered in her eyes. "I just want our boy back."

They sat in the quiet, their helplessness hung heavy in the air, the only comfort they could offer each other was the shared ache of parents who would do anything to take their child's pain away—if only they knew how. Their concern only grew as Kabir continued to struggle, and they longed to reach out and help him find his way through the darkness. Their home became a sanctuary for him, a place where he could seek refuge amidst the chaos of his emotions. Despite their worries, they refused to give up on him, holding onto the hope that he would eventually find his way back to himself.

Kabir stood there, a silent witness to their shared grief, he felt an upsurge of guilt fill him, the realization of the pain he had caused them crashing down upon him like a tidal wave.

And, as he looked upon his parents, their silent suffering laid bare before him, Kabir knew that he could not bear to inflict any more pain upon them, that he could not allow his own selfish desires to overshadow the love and support they had always shown him. And so, with a heavy heart and tears streaming down his cheeks, he made a decision that would change the course of his life forever.

Turning away from the door, Kabir approached his parents with hesitant steps, his voice choked with emotion as he spoke. "Mom, Dad," he whispered, his words barely audible above the soft hum of the night, "I'm sorry. I'm so, so sorry for everything." And as he sank to his knees before them, his heart breaking into a million pieces, he felt their arms wrap around him in a warm embrace, their love and forgiveness a balm to his wounded soul.

As they held each other close, Kabir knew that he had made the right decision. And as he looked into the eyes of his parents, eyes filled with love and understanding, he felt a sense of peace inundate him, the knowledge that he was not alone in his pain, that he had a family who would always be there for him, no matter what. As Kabir clung to his parents, enveloped in their comforting embrace. In that sacred moment of connection, he realized with unwavering certainty that he could no longer allow Maya's presence to poison his heart and soul, nor inflict further pain upon his beloved family.

With tears streaming down his cheeks and his heart heavy with resolve, Kabir made a solemn vow to himself and to his family, he would let go of Maya once and for all, releasing her hold on his heart and soul and banishing her memory from his thoughts forevermore. For he understood now, more than ever, the true cost of holding onto a love that had long since withered and died—a cost that his family had paid dearly in their shared suffering. With a steely determination born of newfound strength, Kabir rose to his feet, his gaze fixed firmly on the future that lay before him.

And as he turned his back on the door that had once represented escape and freedom, he felt a sense of liberation flood him, the weight of Maya's betrayal lifting from his shoulders like a burden too long carried. From that day forward, Kabir walked with his head held high, his heart relieved by the past regrets and lost dreams. And though the road ahead was fraught with uncertainty, he knew that he walked it with the unwavering support of his family by his side, their love and forgiveness a beacon of hope in the darkness of his despair.

In this moment of profound clarity and resolution, Kabir found the strength to let go of Maya and embrace the healing power of moving forward. And as he took his first tentative steps into the unknown, he knew that he was finally free to reclaim his life and his happiness, unencumbered by the chains of the past. From that day forward, Kabir vowed to live each moment with purpose and intention, cherishing the love of his family and embracing the endless possibilities that lay before him. And as he looked towards the future with renewed hope and determination, he knew that he was ready to face whatever challenges lay ahead, secure in the knowledge that he was no longer bound by the shadows of the past. But amongst the self-recrimination and despair, a glimmer of hope remained. Deep down, Kabir knew that he was capable

The Amaranthine Promises: Where love finds its way in the labyrinth of fate, illuminating the path to redemption and renewal. With each page turned, you may find solace in the power of forgiveness and boundless depths of true love.

of more - of love, of joy, of finding happiness once again. And so, with a newfound resolve, he vowed to claw his way out of the darkness and into the light.

Fuelled by the searing rage born from Maya's betrayal, he channelled his pain into a steely resolve. No longer would he allow himself to be consumed by memories of her deceit. Instead, Kabir focused all his energy on self and his family, pouring himself into his aspirations with unwavering dedication. His family became his anchor, providing him with the love and support he needed to weather the storm of Maya's betrayal. Through this journey of self-discovery, Kabir emerged as a man of unwavering resolve, forged in the fires of adversity. He refused to let the past hold him back, choosing instead to harness his pain as a catalyst for growth. With each passing day, he became stronger, more resilient, and more determined to create a future that was free from the shackles of his past.

Kabir began to take the first tentative steps towards healing. He sought out therapy, pouring out his heart to a sympathetic stranger who listened with patience and understanding. He threw himself into his work, channelling his pain into creativity and productivity. And slowly but surely, the fog began to lift. With the support of his friends and family, the world seemed a little brighter, the colours a little more vibrant, the air a little sweeter. Fuelled by a seething rage born from Maya's betrayal, Kabir made a resolute decision to sever all ties with his past. He started by reaching out to his old childhood friends, seeking to mend the bridges that had been burnt in the wake of Maya's deception.

With each heartfelt apology and sincere attempt at reconciliation, Kabir began to rebuild the relationships that had once been torn asunder. However, when it came to his college gang and Maya's family, Kabir harboured an unyielding determination to never look back. The mere thought of them stoked the flames of his fury, reminding him of the pain and heartache they had inflicted upon him. In a defiant act of self-preservation, Kabir vowed to banish them from his thoughts forever, refusing to allow their presence to poison his newfound sense of peace and purpose. It was a cathartic release, a shedding of the past that allowed Kabir to finally move forward unencumbered by the weight of his former life.

With each passing day, Kabir felt the tight grip of grief begin to loosen its grip, replaced by a sense of cautious optimism for the future. But just as he dared to believe that he had finally turned a corner, fate had one final twist in store.

One evening, as Kabir wandered the familiar streets of his neighbourhood, lost in thought, he found himself standing at a familiar crossroads - the spot where he had first Kissed Maya, all those years ago. And as he stood there, bathed in the soft glow of the streetlights, a sense of peace washed over him. Kabir realized that Maya would always be a part of him - a bittersweet memory etched into the fabric of his being, a reminder of love lost, and lessons learned. With a wistful smile, Kabir turned and walked away, leaving behind the ghosts of the past as he stepped boldly into the unknown. For though the road ahead was uncertain, he knew that he was no longer alone - for he carried Family's love with him, a beacon of hope to guide him through the darkest of nights.

The Amaranthine Promises: Where love finds its way in the labyrinth of fate, illuminating the path to redemption and renewal. With each page turned, you may find solace in the power of forgiveness and boundless depths of true love.

In the fiery crucible of betrayal, Kabir emerged reborn, fuelled by a burning determination to forge a new path forward. With rage as the catalyst, he made his peace with his past, seeking redemption not only in the bonds of friendship but also in the embrace of his loving family. With each step, Kabir moved further from the shadows of his former life, embracing the light of a future untainted by the ghosts of betrayal.

The Amaranthine Promises: Where love finds its way in the labyrinth of fate, illuminating the path to redemption and renewal. With each page turned, you may find solace in the power of forgiveness and boundless depths of true love.

Chapter 6
Enchanted Beginnings

As the days stretched into weeks and the weeks into months, Kabir gradually began to emerge from the depths of his despair. With the support of his friends and family, he found solace in the simple pleasures of life - in the laughter of loved ones, the warmth of the sun on his face, and the gentle rhythm of everyday routines.

But amidst the fragile peace of his newfound equilibrium, a new presence entered Kabir's life - one that would irrevocably alter the course of his journey.

Amongst the anarchy and clamour of daily existence, there exists a rare and remarkable soul. To those fortunate enough to know her, she is nothing short of a revelation—a whirlwind of wit, warmth, and boundless generosity, with a heart as vast and vibrant as the universe itself. From the moment she enters a room, she commands attention with her infectious laughter and quicksilver wit, her sharp mind and sharper tongue cutting through the noise of everyday life like a bonfire in the fog. With a smile that could light up the darkest night and a laugh that could melt the hardest heart, she effortlessly captivates all who cross her path, weaving a tapestry of joy and laughter wherever she goes.

The Amaranthine Promises: Where love finds its way in the labyrinth of fate, illuminating the path to redemption and renewal. With each page turned, you may find solace in the power of forgiveness and boundless depths of true love.

But beneath her playful exterior lies a heart of pure gold, overflowing with compassion and kindness. Whether lending a listening ear to those in need or offering a helping hand to those less fortunate, her generosity knew no bounds, her selfless acts of kindness leaving an indelible mark on the lives of all who are touched by her grace. And yet, for all her wit and warmth, there is a depth to this girl that transcends mere words—a quiet strength and resilience born of a lifetime of trials and tribulations. In the face of adversity, she stands tall and unwavering, a symbol of hope and inspiration to all.

Her name was Siya, a colleague at work with a quiet strength and a captivating presence. From the moment they met, there was an instant connection between them - a spark of recognition that transcended mere acquaintance and hinted at deeper, unexplored depths.

Siya was a whirlwind of emotions, a girl whose heart was far too big for her own good. She had this endearing softness about her, the kind that made her cry at the drop of a hat—especially during emotional scenes on TV. It didn't matter if it was a movie, she had seen a hundred times or a simple commercial with a touching moment; her eyes would well up, and she'd reach for a tissue, smiling through her tears as she whispered, "I just can't help it."

Her mornings were a dance of their own. While getting ready for work, the mirror became her stage, and she'd twirl and groove to her favourite songs, humming along as she did her hair. The floor of her room would inevitably be littered with clothes—an entire wardrobe emptied in search of the perfect outfit, only for her to toss it aside and pick something

The Amaranthine Promises: Where love finds its way in the labyrinth of fate, illuminating the path to redemption and renewal. With each page turned, you may find solace in the power of forgiveness and boundless depths of true love.

else entirely at the last minute. It was a routine that her family knew all too well, but it was Siya's way, and they couldn't help but smile at her indecisiveness.

Despite her occasional chaos, Siya's heart was always in the right place. She spent her evenings in the kitchen, helping her mother prepare dinner, always eager to learn new recipes or offer her own twists on the family favourites. And when she wasn't with her mother, she was by her father's side, learning the ropes of the family business. She had a natural knack for it, balancing her work life with the responsibilities at home, always eager to do more, to be more.

Her elder sister adored her, and Siya was her constant companion, always offering advice, a shoulder to cry on, or simply a listening ear. She had this way of making everyone around her feel like they mattered, like they were the most important person in her world when they needed her.

But it was her elder brother who held the softest spot in her heart. He spoiled her endlessly, and she basked in it, knowing that no matter what, he'd always be there for her. Their bond was unbreakable—he was her protector, her confidant, the one who always made her feel safe. And in return, Siya showered him with affection, a love so pure and deep that it was impossible to put into words.

In her quiet moments, when no one was watching, Siya would sit by the window, staring at the sky, her mind filled with dreams and her heart overflowing with love for the people around her. She was the kind of person who carried the weight of others' happiness on her shoulders and never once complained, because that was who she was—compassionate, selfless, and full of life.

In the midst of a busy office, amidst the flurry of new faces and eager introductions, two souls found themselves drawn together by the invisible threads of fate. Kabir and Siya, each embarking on the next chapter of their professional lives, crossed paths for the first time at the induction of their jobs—a moment that would forever alter the course of their destinies. It was Siya's laughter that first caught Kabir's attention—a melodic sound that cut through the hum of conversation like a breath of fresh air. Intrigued by her vivacious spirit and quick wit, Kabir found himself drawn to her side, eager to bask in the warmth of her infectious energy.

And as they exchanged introductions and shared anecdotes of their respective journeys, a spark ignited between them—a spark that would blossom into a bond forged in the fires of mutual understanding and shared purpose. For in each other, Kabir and Siya found not just colleagues, but kindred spirits— two souls united by a common passion and a shared vision for the future.

The induction room was buzzing with the hum of quiet chatter. New joiners were scattered around, nervously flipping through the welcome packets. Kabir sat near the back, fidgeting with a pen, trying to keep calm. He wasn't one to shy away from attention, but this formal environment had him a little on edge. Siya, on the other hand, sat a few rows ahead, looking bright-eyed and curious.

The Amaranthine Promises: Where love finds its way in the labyrinth of fate, illuminating the path to redemption and renewal. With each page turned, you may find solace in the power of forgiveness and boundless depths of true love.

As the HR representative stood at the front, discussing the company's history and values, Kabir's mind drifted. He wasn't paying much attention, but when she asked a question to the room about how the company had evolved, Kabir, without thinking, blurted out, "Well, I'm guessing it got here one email at a time!"

The room fell silent for a second before a burst of uncontrollable laughter echoed from the front. It was Siya, her head thrown back, laughing so hard she could barely breathe. A few others chuckled, but most just looked around, confused. Kabir turned bright red, realizing what he had said.

Siya's laughter was contagious, and soon a few others joined in, but it was her infectious giggles that caught everyone's attention. The HR rep awkwardly cleared her throat, trying to regain control of the room, but Siya couldn't stop, clutching her sides as she laughed. Kabir, now smiling, looked toward her, his embarrassment fading. He couldn't help but be drawn to her carefree spirit.

During the break, Kabir spotted Siya by the coffee machine, still giggling as she recounted the moment to one of her new friends. He hesitated for a second but then decided to approach her.

"Hey, so I guess I'm officially the class clown, huh?" Kabir said with a sheepish grin as he approached Siya.

She looked up, wiping a tear from her eye, still grinning from ear to ear. "Oh my God, that was the best thing I've heard in an induction ever! Who says that in a corporate meeting?"

Kabir shrugged, leaning against the counter. "Apparently, this guy," he said, pointing to himself. "I have a talent for saying the wrong thing at the worst possible time."

Siya burst into laughter again, nearly spilling her coffee. "No, no, it was perfect! I couldn't breathe for a second. You have no idea how much I needed that laugh!"

Kabir laughed along with her, relieved that his blunder had at least made someone's day. "Well, I'm glad my embarrassing moment could be of service. So... are you always this entertained by dumb comments, or was mine just particularly amazing?"

Siya smirked, taking a sip of her coffee. "Let's just say you set a new standard today. I'll be expecting more of that in the future."

"Oh, don't worry," Kabir said, leaning in slightly, "I'm full of dumb comments. It's my secret weapon. Stick around long enough, and you'll be rolling on the floor."

Siya grinned, playfully nudging him. "I might just take you up on that. You're fun."

"You too," Kabir said, feeling more relaxed around her now. "I'm Kabir, by the way."

"Siya," she replied, offering her hand. They shook hands, but Kabir, still feeling cheeky, gave her a mock-serious look.

"So, Siya, tell me—have you mastered the art of pretending to understand all the corporate jargon yet, or are you just as lost as I am?"

The Amaranthine Promises: Where love finds its way in the labyrinth of fate, illuminating the path to redemption and renewal. With each page turned, you may find solace in the power of forgiveness and boundless depths of true love.

Siya giggled, shaking her head. "Oh, I've been nodding and smiling since the presentation started. I'm still trying to figure out what half the acronyms even mean."

Kabir laughed, feeling an instant connection with her. "Same here. Maybe we should form a 'Clueless Club'—meet after work and try to decode corporate speak."

Siya raised an eyebrow, clearly amused. "I'm in. As long as you promise to keep making ridiculous comments during meetings."

Kabir pretended to think it over, then nodded seriously. "Deal. I'll do my best to make a fool of myself at least once a day."

With that, they both laughed, and Kabir realized he'd found someone who shared his sense of humour, someone who could turn even the most awkward moments into something fun. It was the beginning of a friendship—one that had started with a silly comment but was already turning into something more meaningful. And so, in that fateful moment of introduction, Kabir and Siya took their first tentative steps towards a friendship that would defy the odds and transcend the boundaries of time and space. Little did they know, their paths were destined to intertwine in ways they could never have imagined, leading them down a path towards love and fulfilment beyond their wildest dreams.

Siya was drawn to Kabir's magnetic charm and infectious enthusiasm, while Kabir found solace in Siya's steady presence and unwavering support. They quickly became confidants, sharing their hopes, fears, and dreams with one another in whispered conversations and stolen moments of intimacy. In Siya, Kabir found a kindred spirit - someone who understood him in ways that no one else could, who saw past the facade he presented to the world and into the depths of his soul. And in Kabir, Siya found a pillar of strength - a source of comfort and companionship in a world that often felt cold and indifferent. Their friendship blossomed with each passing day, growing stronger and deeper with each shared experience and shared secret. They laughed together, cried together, and navigated the ups and downs of life with a sense of shared purpose and mutual understanding.

It was a quiet afternoon, the kind where conversations naturally turned deeper. Kabir, Siya, and their close friends sat in their favourite café after work. Over time, the group had grown closer, and laughter-filled conversations began to make space for more personal stories.

Kabir sat back in his chair, staring at his coffee cup before deciding to speak. "You know, people don't really understand the things we go through to get where we are," he started, his voice lower than usual.

The group grew quiet, sensing that this was a moment for listening.

"I wasn't always confident," Kabir continued. "Back then, public speaking terrified me. I'd freeze up in class or even just trying to explain something to someone." He paused for a moment, his eyes glancing toward Siya, who watched him closely.

"To force myself out of that fear, I started selling credit cards. I'd go door to door, talking to strangers, getting rejected a hundred times over. People would slam doors in my face or just ignore me completely. But I had no choice but to push through. That job toughened me up."

Siya, sitting just across from him, smiled a little, recognizing the struggles he spoke of. "You know," she said, softly joining the conversation, "I get what you're saying. I had a job selling car insurance a while back. I had to travel long distances every day. It would take me hours to get from one side of the city to the other, and all for peanuts. The job was brutal. Constant rejection, pressure to meet targets, and sometimes even losing my way to places I didn't know."

Kabir looked at her, surprised. "Really? You had to do that?"

Siya nodded, a small laugh escaping her. "Yeah. It wasn't glamorous at all, but it was all I could find at the time. Every day felt like an uphill battle, but I had no choice. I needed to make something of myself. It's funny because just like you, I wasn't the most confident person back then either. I had to learn how to handle rejection pretty quickly."

Kabir's face softened as he heard her story, realizing they had more in common than he thought. "I guess we've both walked that tough road," he said, a sense of understanding passing between them.

"And then," Kabir continued, "my dad's business collapsed. We lost a lot, and things were tough. I had to step up. I started working night shifts at a cyber café—everything from cleaning tables to fixing computers. It wasn't glamorous, but it helped. I'd finish my shift early in the morning and head straight to college, sometimes without any sleep."

Siya's eyes widened. "No sleep and college after a night shift? That must've been brutal."

Kabir nodded, a faint smile on his lips. "Yeah, but it was what I had to do. My family was depending on me. There was no other choice."

Siya's voice softened as she looked at him, the shared understanding growing between them. "It's funny how life throws these things at us. But I think it's what makes us stronger, right? We get through it, somehow."

Kabir met her gaze, a sense of mutual respect between them. "Yeah, you're right. It makes you realize how much you can take."

Their connection deepened as they both reflected on their shared pasts, understanding that they had more in common than just their present. Both had faced hardships, learned resilience, and worked through the struggles that life had thrown at them.

But amidst the warmth and camaraderie of their burgeoning friendship, a shadow loomed on the horizon - the spectre of Kabir's past, lurking just beneath the surface, threatening to disrupt the delicate balance they had worked so hard to achieve. For unbeknownst to Siya, Kabir still carried the scars of his failed relationship with Maya - scars that ran deep and refused to heal, no matter how hard he tried to bury them beneath the veneer of his newfound happiness.

A few days had passed since Kabir and Siya started spending more time together. As they sat in a quieter corner of a nearby café after work, sipping their coffees, the atmosphere felt different—more intimate. The usual banter between them was softer tonight, their connection growing as they found more in common.

Siya glanced at Kabir, sensing there was more to his story. She had heard bits and pieces but never the full truth. Gently, she broke the silence, her curiosity finally getting the better of her.

"Kabir, can I ask you something personal?" Siya's voice was soft but serious.

Kabir, who had been staring into his cup, looked up and nodded. "Yeah, sure. What's on your mind?"

She hesitated for a moment before speaking again. "You mentioned someone before… Maya, right? I can tell it wasn't just any breakup. It seems like it really... broke you."

Kabir's jaw tensed slightly at the mention of Maya's name. He hadn't expected to talk about her, not like this, not with Siya. But something about Siya's genuine concern and the way she looked at him made him feel like it was time to share.

Taking a deep breath, he leaned back and started slowly. "Maya was... everything to me. We were together for years, and I did everything I could to take care of her. I worked all those jobs, juggled night shifts and college just to make sure she had what she needed. I thought we had something special, something that would last forever."

Siya listened intently, her eyes never leaving his. "But?"

Kabir exhaled sharply. "But I was wrong. She... she betrayed me. I caught her with someone else. Not just flirting or talking—she was with him in her apartment, and there was no mistaking what was going on."

Siya's eyes widened slightly, but she remained silent, letting him continue. Kabir's voice tightened as the memories came flooding back. "I thought I was doing everything right, you know? I gave her everything I had, every part of me. And in return, she... she destroyed me. The worst part was, she acted like it was my fault, like I wasn't enough."

Siya reached out and touched his arm gently, her voice filled with empathy. "Kabir, I'm so sorry. That must have been devastating."

Kabir nodded, swallowing hard. "It was. My family stood by me, though, especially my brother, Karan. They were the ones who helped me through it, but it wasn't easy. For the longest time, I blamed myself. I thought maybe if I had done something differently..."

Siya shook her head firmly. "Don't ever think that. People like Maya don't deserve someone like you. You did everything you could, and that's more than enough."

Kabir looked at her, surprised by the strength in her words. He had been drowning in guilt for so long that hearing Siya speak like that was like a lifeline. "Thanks, Siya. I... I needed to hear that."

The Amaranthine Promises: Where love finds its way in the labyrinth of fate, illuminating the path to redemption and renewal. With each page turned, you may find solace in the power of forgiveness and boundless depths of true love.

Siya smiled, squeezing his arm lightly. "Anytime. And for what it's worth, I think you're stronger because of it. You didn't let her break you completely." There was a pause as Kabir nodded, feeling a sense of relief swamp him for the first time in a long while. He looked at Siya, appreciating her presence, her warmth, and the connection they were building.

"So," Siya said after a moment, her tone lighter now, trying to ease the tension. "Did you ever get your revenge? Egg her car or something?"

Kabir chuckled softly, shaking his head. "No, nothing like that. But I'd be lying if I said it didn't cross my mind."

They both laughed, the heavy moment giving way to a sense of ease between them. Kabir felt a shift inside him—a new chapter beginning, with Siya by his side.

And as their friendship deepened into something more, Kabir found himself torn between the past and the present, between the ghost of a love lost and the promise of a love yet to be discovered. But, amidst the turmoil of his inner conflict, one thing remained clear - his feelings for Siya were undeniable, immutable, irrevocable. And though he knew the road ahead would be fraught with uncertainty and peril, he vowed to tread it with courage and conviction, guided by the light of love that burned bright within his heart. For in Siya, Kabir had found not only a friend, but a confidant, a companion, a soulmate. And though the journey ahead would be fraught with challenges and obstacles, he knew that with Siya by his side, anything was possible.

The Amaranthine Promises: Where love finds its way in the labyrinth of fate, illuminating the path to redemption and renewal. With each page turned, you may find solace in the power of forgiveness and boundless depths of true love.

*As Kabir emerges from the shadows of his own despair,
he finds himself drawn to a new beginning—a chance encounter with
Siya, a beacon of light amidst the darkness. In her presence,
Kabir discovers a renewed sense of hope. This chapter revealed the
growing bond between Kabir and Siya, both shaped by their struggles.
Through shared stories of hardship and perseverance, they connected on
a deeper level, finding comfort in each other's experiences. Kabir's painful
past with Maya, and Siya's relentless pursuit of her own dreams,
highlighted how challenges can forge resilience—and how opening up to
someone can lead to unexpected healing.*

The Amaranthine Promises: Where love finds its way in the labyrinth of fate,
illuminating the path to redemption and renewal. With each page turned, you may
find solace in the power of forgiveness and boundless depths of true love.

Chapter 7
Laughter Under the Moonlight

Kabir and his colleagues were lounging around in the break room one afternoon, throwing ideas back and forth about how to blow off some steam after a particularly intense month at work. Someone joked about taking a day off to stay home and sleep, while another suggested hitting a bar for drinks. But Kabir, half-laughing, threw in, "Why not do something a bit crazier? Like a road trip?"

The room buzzed with enthusiasm at his suggestion, with everyone chiming in all at once. Siya, sitting at the corner, raised an eyebrow with a playful grin and said, "Road trip? With this lot? I'm not sure we'd make it back alive!" The others laughed, but Kabir caught her eye and said, "C'mon, where's your spirit? It'll be fun! We'll put you in charge of the music!"

A few colleagues groaned in mock horror, knowing Siya's questionable playlist of old-school romantic songs, while Siya laughed out loud, "You'd regret that decision within ten minutes, Kabir. I'm warning you!"

One of the team members, Naveen, chimed in, "Fine, road trip it is! But who's planning this? If it's Siya, expect detours every few kilometers for her to take selfies," teasing her for her notorious love for photos.

Siya shot back, "Only if you carry my bags, Naveen!"

The Amaranthine Promises: Where love finds its way in the labyrinth of fate, illuminating the path to redemption and renewal. With each page turned, you may find solace in the power of forgiveness and boundless depths of true love.

By the end of the conversation, everyone was on board, agreeing to set a date soon. But what was undeniable was the excitement growing between Kabir and Siya, their banter and connection forming the heartbeat of the group's upcoming adventure.

The air buzzed with excitement as Kabir and Siya, along with their office colleagues, embarked on a weekend trip to a scenic resort. The anticipation hung heavy in the air as they piled into the bus, their laughter mingling with the hum of engines as they set off on their adventure.

As everyone gathered near the office entrance for the road trip, there was a sense of excitement in the air. People were busy chatting, organizing their bags, and securing their seats on the bus. Siya, quick on her feet, had already snagged a seat near the window and sneakily placed her bag on the one next to her, saving it for Kabir.

The bus started to fill up quickly, and Siya, with a knowing smile, kept looking out the door, waiting for Kabir to arrive. When he finally showed up, a few minutes late, he noticed Siya waving at him with a mischievous glint in her eyes, clearly signalling that she had saved him a seat. But Kabir, being playful, pretended not to notice. Instead, he went straight to the back of the bus and plopped down with some of the guys, ignoring her.

Siya's smile faded as she watched him settle in with the others. One of her colleagues, noticing the empty seat, tried to sit next to her, but she quickly stopped them, saying, "That seat's taken!" She was now visibly irritated, her excitement dulled by Kabir's playful snub.

As the bus started moving, Kabir could feel the cold stare from Siya even from the back. He shot a few glances her way, but she wasn't having it. After about 30 minutes of regret and awkward laughter with the guys, Kabir finally stood up, realizing he had pushed his luck too far.

Walking down the aisle, he approached her, leaning over the back of her seat. "Hey, someone sitting here?" he asked, trying to sound innocent, but she ignored him and looked out the window.

Feigning defeat, Kabir sat on the floor beside her seat, his back against the chair, and said dramatically, "I guess I deserve the floor, huh?"

Siya crossed her arms, still fuming but amused by his antics. He grinned up at her and added, "I'll make it up to you... I'll let you choose the music."

She finally cracked a smile, though still pretending to be mad. "Oh, you're definitely making it up. You'll be my personal DJ for the entire trip!"

Kabir got up, sliding into the seat next to her with a relieved smile. "Deal. Now, where's that playlist of tragic songs?"

Siya laughed out loud, giving in completely, and the tension dissolved as they resumed their usual playful banter. The rest of the trip was filled with jokes, teasing, and the shared connection they had built over time.

The Amaranthine Promises: Where love finds its way in the labyrinth of fate, illuminating the path to redemption and renewal. With each page turned, you may find solace in the power of forgiveness and boundless depths of true love.

As the bus meandered through the winding mountain roads, the atmosphere inside had shifted from casual chatter to quiet awe. The scenery outside was breath-taking—lush green valleys stretching out below them, mist clinging to the peaks of distant mountains. Streams glistened as they cascaded down the rocky slopes, and the air, crisp and cool, was filled with the scent of pine and earth. The road seemed to disappear into the horizon, with towering trees and wildflowers lining the path.

Their destination was a remote resort nestled amidst rolling hills and verdant forests, a tranquil oasis far removed from the hustle and bustle of city life. When they finally arrived at their destination, a beautiful old bungalow stood before them, nestled in the heart of the valley, surrounded by vibrant gardens and towering trees. The white stone structure was classic yet charming, with a rustic wooden porch wrapping around the front. Ivy crept up the sides of the building, giving it a fairy-tale-like appearance. The bungalow sat on the edge of a cliff, offering panoramic views of the valleys below and the distant mountain range, which seemed to stretch endlessly across the horizon.

The group was silent for a moment, taking in the sheer beauty of the place. "This… is unbelievable," Siya whispered, her eyes wide as she looked around.

The rooms inside the bungalow were cozy and inviting, each with large windows that opened out to spectacular views of the mountains and valleys below. Kabir's room had a balcony, and as he stepped out, he was greeted by the sight of the sun beginning to dip behind the mountains, casting

The Amaranthine Promises: Where love finds its way in the labyrinth of fate, illuminating the path to redemption and renewal. With each page turned, you may find solace in the power of forgiveness and boundless depths of true love.

a golden glow across the landscape. The sky was a mixture of soft pinks, oranges, and purples, and the valley below was bathed in the warm light of dusk.

Siya's room, just next door, offered an awe-inspiring view. From her window, she could see a tranquil lake in the distance, reflecting the colours of the sunset like a mirror. Birds flitted across the sky, heading to their nests as the day turned into night.

They both stood silently at their respective windows, taking in the beauty of it all, completely in awe of how perfect the place was. It felt surreal—like they had stumbled upon a hidden paradise tucked away from the world. The peacefulness of the surroundings was the perfect antidote to the chaos of their usual city lives.

"This is going to be one unforgettable trip," Kabir muttered to himself, still gazing out at the view, lost in the serenity of the moment.

The first night of the weekend getaway found the group gathered around a crackling campfire, the blazes casting flickering shadows across their faces as they laughed and shared stories late into the night. Kabir couldn't shake the feeling of unease that gnawed at him as he watched other men from their group vying for Siya's attention, their eyes lingering a little too long on her beauty.

As the flames crackled and laughter filled the air, Kabir sat silently, his eyes scanning the group. The introductions had been light-hearted at first, but he couldn't help but notice how several of the guys seemed to be paying extra attention to Siya.

One of them even made a joke about trying his luck with her, and Kabir's chest tightened with jealousy. He tried to brush it off, but the feeling gnawed at him, making it impossible to enjoy the evening. The conversations continued and a surge of jealousy coursed through Kabir's veins as he observed the interactions, his heart pounding in his chest as he struggled to keep his emotions in check.

Unable to take it any longer, he glanced over at Siya, who was laughing at something another guy said. Without thinking, he leaned closer and whispered, "Siya, fancy a walk?"

Siya looked up, a little surprised, but nodded with a smile. "Sure." her eyes grateful, as they slid away from the group and into the darkness beyond the reach of the campfire's glow. The air was heavy with tension as they walked in silence, each lost in their own thoughts. Unnoticed by most, and wandered down a small path that led away from the noise of the group. The moon hung low in the sky, casting a soft, silvery glow over the landscape. The air was cool, and the only sounds were the rustling of leaves and their footsteps on the soft ground.

For a few minutes, they walked in silence, the tautness between them palpable. Finally, as they reached a secluded spot Kabir broke the silence. "So... you seem to be popular tonight," he said, his voice tight with the jealousy he was trying hard to suppress.

Siya glanced sideways at him, catching the hint of frustration in his tone. "Oh? And what does that mean?"

Kabir sighed, rubbing the back of his neck as he searched for the right words. "I just... I don't like it when other guys act like that around you. It bothers me, more than I thought it would." Kabir turned to Siya, his heart racing with a mixture of fear and longing. "I can't stand seeing other guys look at you like that," he confessed, his voice thick with emotion. "It drives me crazy."

Siya stopped walking and turned to face him, her eyes softened with understanding her expression demulcent. "Kabir, you don't have to worry about them. I'm not interested in anyone else." She paused, her voice lowering as she added, "If you haven't noticed, I only care about you. You're the only one I see."

Her words sent a wave of warmth through him, calming the jealousy that had been simmering beneath the surface. "I guess I just don't want to lose you," he admitted, his eyes meeting hers in the moonlight. "You mean more to me than I can even put into words."

Siya stepped closer, her hand brushing lightly against his arm as she smiled. "You won't lose me, Kabir. I'm right here, aren't I?"

For a moment, they stood there under the moonlit sky, the world around them falling away. Kabir reached out and gently took her hand, their fingers intertwining as they continued their walk in silence, the tension between them replaced with something far deeper—an unspoken understanding of what they meant to each other.

As they strolled through the quiet night, the silver light of the moon reflected in Siya's eyes, and Kabir couldn't help but feel like everything in that moment was perfect. For in Siya's

The Amaranthine Promises: Where love finds its way in the labyrinth of fate, illuminating the path to redemption and renewal. With each page turned, you may find solace in the power of forgiveness and boundless depths of true love.

eyes, he found the truth he had been searching for - a love that was steadfast and true.

He squeezed her hand, pulling her a little closer, as if afraid the night might slip away too quickly. "This... this is all I want," he said softly, "just you and me, like this."

Siya smiled, leaning her head against his shoulder as they walked. "Me too, Kabir. Me too."

The next morning, the group set out to explore the nearby caves. The air was crisp, and excitement buzzed as everyone geared up for the adventure. As they ventured deeper into the cavernous depths, Kabir couldn't shake the feeling of unease that gripped him once more. When they reached the rocky terrain near the cave entrance, Kabir noticed someone else from the group—a tall guy who had been chatty the night before—offering his hand to help Siya navigate the uneven path.

Kabir's chest tightened as he watched, a familiar surge of jealousy running through his veins. His first instinct was to step in, to shield her, to claim her attention. But then, as he stood there, a new thought struck him— something deeper, more reflective than the raw emotion that usually surfaced in moments like this.

It wasn't really about the guy offering his hand, was it? Kabir realized it was his own fear. Fear rooted in the scars left by Maya, and the way she had left him broken, choosing someone else over the love he had given her. For so long, that wound had festered, and any hint of another man's attention toward someone he cared about felt like a reopening of that painful chapter.

But today, as Kabir stood on those rocks, watching Siya politely smile and decline the offer for help, something shifted in him. He wasn't with Maya anymore. This wasn't the past. Siya wasn't Maya. And he wasn't the same person he had been back then. He had grown, had faced the heartbreak, and was standing here now with a choice: to cling to the fear, or to trust again.

As the wind brushed his face and the morning sun warmed his skin, Kabir took a deep breath. This is different, he told himself. Siya deserves more than the shadow of my past, and so do I.

He realized that love required more than just affection—it needed faith. Faith in the person standing beside him, and faith in himself that he could love without being crippled by insecurity. Instead of letting his past dictate his actions, he decided to trust. To let Siya make her choices without his fear clouding everything.

Kabir smiled to himself as he walked up to where Siya was waiting, her eyes lighting up when she saw him. He reached for her hand—not out of jealousy, but simply because he wanted to share the moment with her. As their fingers intertwined, Kabir felt a calmness settle over him, a quiet but profound realization that maybe—just maybe—he could open his heart again.

And this time, he wouldn't let fear hold him back.

The Amaranthine Promises: Where love finds its way in the labyrinth of fate, illuminating the path to redemption and renewal. With each page turned, you may find solace in the power of forgiveness and boundless depths of true love.

As they emerged from the cave into the warm embrace of the morning sun, Kabir turned to Siya with a newfound sense of clarity. "Siya," he said, his voice trembling with emotion, "I love you."

Siya's eyes widened in surprise, her hand flying to her mouth in shock. But then, a smile spread across her face, lighting up her features with a radiant glow.

"I love you too, Kabir," she whispered, her voice barely above a whisper. "I've loved you all along."

And, amidst the quiet intimacy of their shared space, Kabir felt a sense of peace and contentment he had never known. For in Siya's arms, he had found his home, his anchor, his guiding light in a world filled with uncertainty.

In the glow of the moonlight, Kabir and Siya find solace in each other's laughter, forging a bond that transcends the trials of the past. As they dance beneath the stars, they embrace the joy of the present moment, savouring the simple pleasures of companionship and camaraderie.

The Amaranthine Promises: Where love finds its way in the labyrinth of fate, illuminating the path to redemption and renewal. With each page turned, you may find solace in the power of forgiveness and boundless depths of true love.

Chapter 8
Ghosts of the Past

As Kabir and Siya returned from their weekend getaway, a newfound sense of clarity enveloped them. The journey back home was filled with shared glances and tender touches, each moment reinforcing the deep connection they had discovered within each other.

Back at work, Kabir found himself approaching each day with renewed vigour and purpose. His interactions with Siya took on a new depth, their conversations laced with an unspoken understanding and affection that seemed to grow with each passing moment.

Kabir found himself standing in front of the mirror, adjusting his tie for the third time that morning. He sighed, ran his hand through his hair, and muttered, "Come on, man, you've got this." Since he'd set his sights on her, his entire routine had shifted. Morning jogs, which he once despised, were now sacred rituals. His wardrobe, once dominated by shades of grey and blue, now featured colours that popped – reds, yellows, even a daring lavender shirt he never thought he'd wear.

Each day was an unspoken challenge, a little mission to catch her attention. Whether it was his meticulously styled hair or his choice of cologne that lingered just long enough as he walked past her desk, Kabir was trying everything.

But it was never enough, at least not in his mind. One morning, Kabir showed up at work in a crisp white shirt and pants that almost made him feel overdressed. His colleague, who was sipping on his morning coffee, looked up and couldn't help but grin.

"Who are you trying to impress, dude? Got a meeting with the Queen?"

Kabir rolled his eyes but glanced subtly at her across the room. She was laughing at something Sarah had said, completely oblivious to his outfit, his new cologne, or the fact that he'd done an extra set of crunches that morning.

"Just... trying to stay sharp, you know?" Kabir mumbled, trying to play it cool.

His colleague chuckled, "Right, because working out and wearing pastels is so you."

Kabir couldn't help but laugh at himself. "Hey, you never know, man. Maybe she likes guys who look... put together."

His colleague shook his head, still smiling. "Or maybe she just likes guys who don't try too hard."

Kabir leaned back in his chair, pretending to be deep in thought. "Maybe, but until then... pass me that protein shake."

Amidst the blissful haze of newfound love, a nagging doubt lingered in the back of Kabir's mind. He couldn't shake the feeling that he was unworthy of Siya's love, that his past

The Amaranthine Promises: Where love finds its way in the labyrinth of fate, illuminating the path to redemption and renewal. With each page turned, you may find solace in the power of forgiveness and boundless depths of true love.

mistakes and insecurities would inevitably drive her away. As the days turned into weeks, Kabir found himself grappling with his inner demons, the gravity of his past pulling him down with relentless force. He couldn't escape the memories of his failed relationships, the wounds still raw and tender despite the passage of time. Siya, ever perceptive, sensed the turmoil brewing within Kabir's heart. She reached out to him with gentle words of reassurance, her touch a soothing balm on his troubled soul. But try as she might, she couldn't erase the doubts that plagued him, the fear of repeating past mistakes looming large in his mind.

One evening, as they sat together in the quiet comfort of Kabir's apartment, he found himself laying bare his deepest fears to Siya.

Kabir sat on the balcony, the night breeze ruffling his hair as he stared out into the city lights. The quiet hum of the city below seemed to mirror the storm of thoughts in his head. Siya noticed his silence, the way he had been retreating into himself for the past few days. She gently walked over, sitting down beside him, her warmth close but not overwhelming.

"Hey, you've been really quiet lately," she said softly, placing her hand on his. "Is everything okay?"

Kabir hesitated, his eyes fixed on the skyline. For a moment, he wondered if he could really put his fears into words. But then, with Siya by his side, his chest was filled with a little more confidence than before.

"I don't know," he started, his voice barely above a whisper. "It's just…sometimes, I feel like no matter how much I try, the

The Amaranthine Promises: Where love finds its way in the labyrinth of fate, illuminating the path to redemption and renewal. With each page turned, you may find solace in the power of forgiveness and boundless depths of true love.

past keeps coming back. Like I'm constantly being pulled into things I thought I'd moved on from."

Siya listened, her expression calm, her hand squeezing his gently. She didn't interrupt, just let him speak.

"I've made mistakes, Siya," he continued, his words more strained now. "Things I wish I could take back, decisions I regret. And I can't help but think… what if they define me? What if… I never really escape them?"

He looked at her then, his eyes filled with a vulnerability that he had kept hidden for too long. "What if you can't trust me… what if I can't trust myself?"

Siya turned to face him fully, her eyes searching his face, seeing the fear and pain he had kept inside. She took a deep breath, her voice steady but full of warmth.

"Kabir, the past is just that – the past," she said gently. "It doesn't get to decide who you are today, and it certainly doesn't get to define what we have. You're not that person anymore. You've grown, you've learned, and I trust you."

He looked down, "But what if it's not enough?"

Siya smiled softly, lifting his chin so he could meet her gaze. "It is enough. You are enough. We all have things we wish we could change, but that doesn't mean we're bound by them. The only thing that matters now is how you move forward, how we move forward—together."

Kabir's eyes softened, but doubt still lingered. "But what if I mess up again? What if…" "Then we deal with it,"

The Amaranthine Promises: Where love finds its way in the labyrinth of fate, illuminating the path to redemption and renewal. With each page turned, you may find solace in the power of forgiveness and boundless depths of true love.

Siya interrupted, her tone firm but loving. "We don't run. We don't hide. We face it, just like we're facing this now. You don't need to be perfect, Kabir. You just need to trust yourself and trust me."

Her words sank deep into his heart, and for the first time in what felt like weeks, Kabir felt a sense of calm deluge him. The fear, though still there, wasn't as overwhelming. It didn't hold the same power it once did.

"I've been so afraid of losing you," he admitted quietly. Siya leaned in closer, her forehead resting gently against his. "You're not going to lose me. Not unless you push me away."

Kabir closed his eyes, a small smile playing on his lips. "I don't want to do that. Not anymore."

Siya smiled back, her voice soft and reassuring. "Good, because I'm not going anywhere. The past stays where it belongs—behind us. You just need to trust in the love we have right now."

For a long moment, they stayed like that, the silence between them no longer heavy, but peaceful. Kabir finally exhaled, feeling the tightness in his chest begin to ease.

"Thank you," he whispered.

Siya smiled, brushing a hand through his hair. "Anytime. You're stuck with me, remember?"

Kabir chuckled softly, his heart feeling lighter than it had in days. "I wouldn't have it any other way."

To his surprise and relief, Siya's response was one of unwavering love and support. She held him close, her arms a sanctuary against the storm raging within him, her words a beacon of hope in the darkness.

"Kabir," she whispered, her voice soft and reassuring, "you are not defined by your past. You are a kind, loving, and compassionate man, and I am grateful every day to have you in my life."

As they held each other close, Kabir felt a weight lift from his shoulders, replaced by a sense of peace and acceptance he had never known. For in Siya's love, he found the strength to confront his demons, to face his fears head-on and emerge stronger on the other side.

From that day forward, Kabir vowed to cherish every moment he shared with Siya, to never take her love for granted, and to strive each day to be the man she deserved. And as they embarked on the next chapter of their journey together, hand in hand, Kabir knew that with Siya by his side, anything was possible.

Months drifted by like whispers on the wind, carrying with them the echoes of a past stained by betrayal and deceit. For Maya, the time had been a cruel mistress, her path marred by the consequences of her own actions. She had everything she ever desired—wealth, status, and power— but in the depths of her heart, she knew that true happiness had always eluded her.

As Maya walked the corridors of her opulent mansion, the emptiness of her existence weighed heavily upon her soul. Her husband, though wealthy and influential, offered her no solace, his love a distant memory lost to the passage of time. Her days were filled with hollow pursuits and shallow pleasures, her nights haunted by the spectre of loneliness and regret.

And then, like a ghost from the past, Kabir reappeared in her life, his presence a reminder of the love she had lost and the mistakes she could never undo. In his eyes, she saw the reflection of her own guilt, the silent accusation of a heart betrayed.

Kabir stepped into the busy café, distracted by his thoughts, intending to grab a quick coffee before heading home. He had no plans for the evening, just a quiet night of reflection. But as fate would have it, the past had other ideas.

His eyes fell on her—Maya, sitting at a corner table, staring blankly into her cup. His heart froze for a moment, the memory of their turbulent past hitting him hard. He hadn't seen her in months. But before he could turn and leave unnoticed, she looked up and their eyes locked.

"Kabir..." she breathed, the surprise in her voice unmistakable.

Kabir's jaw clenched, but there was no escaping now. He approached her table slowly, standing there for a second too long, debating whether to say anything at all. But she motioned toward the seat in front of her.

"Please... sit," she said, her voice tinged with desperation.

Reluctantly, Kabir sat down, keeping his distance emotionally even though physically he was mere inches away. The silence between them was heavy, the weight of years unspoken sitting like a stone between them. He stared at her, waiting for her to speak first.

Maya shifted nervously, her hands playing with the edge of her cup. "I... I didn't expect to see you here."

"I didn't expect to see you either," Kabir replied, his tone cold, giving nothing away.

She bit her lip, trying to gather her thoughts. "I've been meaning to reach out... but I didn't know if you'd even talk to me."

Kabir raised an eyebrow, leaning back slightly. "You were right. I wouldn't."

Maya flinched at his bluntness but pushed forward. "Kabir, I know I hurt you. I know I pushed you away when all you did was care about me. I... I regret it. I've been regretting it every day."

He crossed his arms, his face hard. "Regret doesn't change the past, Maya."

She swallowed, her voice trembling. "No, it doesn't. But... but things have changed for me. My marriage... it's over. It's been falling apart. My husband—he's never treated me the way you did. He never made me feel... loved. I never should've left you. I should've fought for what we had."

Kabir's eyes narrowed, his voice low and sharp. "You made your choice, Maya. You walked away from me. And now, you think you can just come back because your life didn't turn out the way you wanted?"

The Amaranthine Promises: Where love finds its way in the labyrinth of fate, illuminating the path to redemption and renewal. With each page turned, you may find solace in the power of forgiveness and boundless depths of true love.

Maya's eyes filled with desperation. "No, it's not like that. I realize now that you were the one who truly cared. You were the one who... who loved me. I missed that. I missed you, Kabir."

Desperate for redemption, Maya sought forgiveness from Kabir, her words a plea for absolution in a world tainted by her own greed and ambition. But as she reached out to him, hoping to mend the shattered pieces of their fractured relationship, she realized the true extent of her folly.

She reached out to touch his hand, but he pulled it back sharply, his gaze hard as steel.

"Don't," he said coldly. "Don't you dare."

Maya's voice cracked, her emotions spilling over. "I made a mistake, Kabir. I know that now. But can't we... I don't know... pick up where we left off? I know it sounds crazy, but I've never stopped thinking about you. I've never stopped wanting you."

Kabir's face twisted with disgust, and he stood up abruptly, towering over her. "Pick up where we left off? You really think that after all this time, after everything you did, I would entertain that thought for even a second?"

Maya blinked, tears welling up in her eyes. "Kabir, please—"

"No, Maya," he cut her off, his voice harsh and unrelenting. "You left me because you thought the grass was greener on the other side. You wanted more, something better, and now that you realize you lost it, you come crawling back? Do you think I'm that weak?"

Her lip trembled, and she whispered, "I'm sorry..."

Kabir leaned in closer, his words biting. "Sorry isn't enough. You shattered something that can't be fixed. You can't just show up and expect me to forget the pain, the betrayal, the way you tossed me aside like I was nothing."

Maya shook her head, tears spilling down her cheeks. "I... I didn't know what I was doing. I thought—"

"You thought wrong," Kabir snapped, his anger rising. "You thought I'd wait around forever, didn't you? But let me be clear, Maya, I will never forget what you did. And I will never forgive you."

His final words hung in the air like a knife, cutting through whatever hope Maya had left. She looked up at him, broken and defeated, realizing for the first time that this wasn't just a conversation—it was the end.

Kabir turned on his heel without another word, walking away from her and the café, leaving Maya behind in the ruins of her regrets.

For Kabir had moved on, his heart no longer bound by the chains of the past. In Siya, he had found a love that was pure and true, a love that had healed the wounds left by Maya's betrayal. And as he stood before her, his gaze unwavering and his words filled with resolve, Maya understood the depth of her own folly.

Like gazing into the mirror, Maya saw herself for who she truly was—a woman consumed by her own desires, willing to sacrifice everything for the sake of her own selfish ambitions. And as her sins bore down upon her, she knew that there could be no redemption, no forgiveness for the choices she had made.

With a heavy heart and a soul burdened by regret, Maya turned away from Kabir, her dreams of reconciliation shattered by the harsh reality of her own actions. And as she retreated into the shadows of her lonely existence, she knew that she would carry the scars of her betrayal for the rest of her days.

For Kabir, Maya's final words were a bittersweet reminder of the pain she had inflicted, a solemn vow never to forget and never to forgive. And as he watched her disappear into the darkness, he felt a sense of closure sinking in, a newfound understanding of the true nature of love and forgiveness.

In Siya's arms, he found solace and strength, her love a beacon of hope in a world darkened by the shadows of the past. And as they walked hand in hand into the embrace of their future, Kabir knew that he had finally found peace, his heart free from the chains of regret and resentment. For sometimes, the greatest lessons in life are learned not through forgiveness, but through the power of letting go. And as Kabir gazed into Siya's eyes, he knew that their love was a gift—a blessing in disguise that had guided him through the darkness and into the light.

The Amaranthine Promises: Where love finds its way in the labyrinth of fate, illuminating the path to redemption and renewal. With each page turned, you may find solace in the power of forgiveness and boundless depths of true love.

In this powerful and emotionally charged chapter, Kabir unexpectedly encounters Maya, his ex who regrets the way she ended their relationship. Maya, now stuck in a failed marriage, seeks redemption and attempts to rekindle her past with Kabir, longing for the love and care she once received from him. However, Kabir refuses to entertain her advances, brutally shutting down her hopes for reconciliation. In a confrontation filled with raw honesty, Kabir makes it clear that while the past may haunt them both, he will never forgive or forget the pain she caused, leaving Maya to face the harsh reality of her mistakes.

The Amaranthine Promises: Where love finds its way in the labyrinth of fate, illuminating the path to redemption and renewal. With each page turned, you may find solace in the power of forgiveness and boundless depths of true love.

Chapter 9
The Haunted Inn

The excitement for Kabir and Siya's first solo road trip began to build long before the trip was even planned. It had started innocuously enough—over coffee one evening after work, when they had casually mentioned how both of them had always wanted to take a spontaneous road trip. No itineraries, no big group, just the open road, and the thrill of discovery.

"I've never really had a road trip like that," Siya had confessed, her eyes sparkling with the idea. "You know, just driving wherever the road takes you, stopping wherever you feel like, no fixed plans."

Kabir's interest was piqued. He smiled, leaning forward. "Same here. I mean, I've travelled a lot, but there's something special about the idea of no plans, no pressure. Just us, the car, and the road."

That idea grew quickly in their minds, taking on a life of its own. What started as a light conversation turned into nightly discussions about the places they could go—mountains, beaches, scenic routes, hidden cafes along the way. The more they talked about it, the more Kabir felt a bubbling excitement rising within him. The idea of being on the road with Siya, just the two of them, felt like the perfect way to break away from the routine, the stress of their daily lives, and truly connect. The spontaneity of the plan was what made it even more exciting. They both agreed that this trip was going to be different from anything they'd done before—no prebooked accommodations, no rigid schedules. They'd decide things as they went, depending on where the road took them.

One evening, over a late-night call, Siya had said with a laugh, "I'm ready when you are. Let's just go for it. It's our chance to get lost and not care for once."

Kabir's heart had skipped a beat at that. The thought of the two of them driving down unknown roads, playing their favourite music, sharing stories, and discovering hidden spots together—it all sounded perfect. There was a sense of freedom in it that excited him like nothing else.

So, they set the plan in motion. They chose a weekend and decided to pack lightly—just essentials. "We'll figure things out on the go," Kabir had said, grinning.

The countdown to their road trip began, and with every passing day, Kabir felt his excitement growing. It wasn't just about the destination—it was about the journey, the adventure, and the feeling of sharing it all with Siya.

With each passing day, Kabir couldn't help but think about how much this meant to him. It wasn't just their first trip together—it was the beginning of something new, something unplanned and unpredictable, but full of promise. The road ahead was calling, and for once, they both couldn't wait to get lost.

As they neared the day of the trip, both Kabir and Siya were caught in their own whirlwinds of thoughts and emotions.

For Kabir, it was the thrill of finally being able to spend some uninterrupted time with Siya. He couldn't help but think of how much fun they would have, laughing over silly jokes, singing along to their favourite songs, and discovering new places together. But, amidst all the excitement, a deeper, quieter thought kept surfacing. This was their first trip alone— just the two of them. As much as the adventure excited him, Kabir couldn't deny that he was also thinking about how close they'd be. The long drives, the shared spaces—there was something intimate about the whole experience, something that made his heart race in anticipation.

Siya, on the other hand, found herself in a delicate mix of excitement and nervousness. She had always been independent, never hesitating to explore the world around her, but this was different. It was the first time she was going on a trip alone with a guy, and not just any guy—Kabir. She liked him, more than she had let on to herself. And now, they'd be spending days together, alone. Her heart fluttered at the thought.

As Siya packed for the trip, she stood in front of her wardrobe, trying to decide what to bring. The thought of what Kabir might think when he saw her in something more relaxed, more personal, kept crossing her mind. Would he notice? What would he say if he saw her in that delicate nightwear, she had kept aside? It wasn't provocative, but it was soft, beautiful, and feminine. She could almost imagine his eyes lighting up when he saw her after a long day of driving, unwinding under the stars. There was a quiet kind of romance in the air already, and Siya felt both excited and nervous about what the nights might bring.

The thought lingered—would they stay up late, talking under the stars, sharing things they hadn't yet told each other? What if Kabir's gaze held onto hers a little too long? Would he reach out for her hand as they sat together, perhaps even pull her close? These thoughts sent a gentle shiver down her spine, not out of fear but anticipation of what could unfold between them. There was a certain electricity between them, and this trip felt like it could take them to a place they had both been hesitating to go.

But amidst all the excitement, she trusted Kabir. That's what made her nervous thoughts turn into something sweeter—she knew, deep down, that he respected her, that he would never push her into something she wasn't ready for. That made her feel safe, even as her heart raced thinking about the possibilities. Would he make a move, or would they both remain in this playful tension for a little longer?

They both shared a common thought, though in their own way—this trip was not just about the adventure, it was about testing new waters, seeing where their connection would lead them. For Kabir, it was about taking a step closer to Siya. For Siya, it was about seeing if they could bridge the gap between their relationship and something more, all while wrapped in the magic of the journey ahead.

Kabir and Siya embarked on their much-anticipated road trip, excitement swirling in the air between them as they ventured into the heart of the countryside. The open road stretched out before them, the city slowly giving way to the rolling hills and valleys. With the windows rolled down, the cool breeze rushed in, carrying with it the scent of distant pine trees. Their favourite songs blared from the speakers, creating the perfect soundtrack to their adventure—an upbeat mix of classic rock and some cheesy pop tunes that made them both laugh as they sang along, carefree and happy.

Kabir glanced over at Siya as she danced playfully in her seat, her hair tousled by the wind. She caught him smiling and threw a chip at him from the bag of snacks she had been munching on. "Eyes on the road, driver!" she teased, laughing as Kabir swerved slightly, playfully pretending to lose control. He reached into the bag, grabbing a handful of chips, retaliating with a grin.

After hours of driving, their bellies started to rumble, so they decided to make a pit stop. Pulling into a small roadside diner, they ordered burgers and fries, and Siya insisted on getting milkshakes—because, as she said, "What's a road trip without milkshakes?" They sat at a worn wooden table under a large tree, watching as other travellers passed by. The conversation flowed effortlessly, full of jokes, shared stories, and plans for what they'd do once they reached their destination.

Back on the road, the sun began to set, casting a golden hue across the horizon. The drive became quieter, more reflective as the miles slipped by. They watched the changing scenery through tired eyes, the highway now nearly empty, winding through the desolate countryside. The music still played softly in the background, but the energy had shifted into something more serene.

As they continued down the darkening road, they stumbled upon something unexpected—a large, weather-beaten inn, standing eerily still in the shadows just off the highway. Its ancient stone façade was covered in creeping ivy, its windows dark and ominous. Kabir slowed the car as they approached, both of them staring at the old building in silence. "Is this our stop for the night?" Siya asked, half-joking, but her curiosity piqued as well.

"It looks... interesting," Kabir said with a hint of sarcasm, but his eyes twinkled with intrigue.

"Let's just check it out," Siya added, leaning forward to get a better look at the towering inn as they parked in front of it. They had driven for hours, and their bodies were starting to feel the fatigue of the long journey. A place to rest, even one that looked like it had seen better days, seemed like a good idea.

With their bags slung over their shoulders, they stepped out of the car and walked toward the massive wooden doors. The inn loomed above them, silent and ominous. Kabir pushed open the creaky door, and they were greeted by the scent of old wood and dust, the dim lighting casting long shadows across the vast entrance hall. The place seemed nearly deserted, except for an old man behind the reception desk, who looked up at them with a knowing smile that sent a chill down their spines.

As they stepped inside, a chill wind whispered through the corridors, sending shivers down their spines. "This looks like something straight out of a horror movie," Siya whispered, half excited, half nervous.

Kabir nodded, but despite the eerie vibe, they were both too tired to care. They exchanged a quick look, shrugged, and decided to stay. After all, it was all part of the adventure, right?

Ignoring the foreboding atmosphere, Kabir completed the check-in formalities while Siya retreated to their room, her heart pounding in her chest. The room, a cozy yet worn-out space with a large window that overlooked the vast, dark forest surrounding the inn. As they settled in, the exhaustion of the day caught up with them, and despite the eerie atmosphere, they couldn't help but feel a sense of strange comfort. The old inn, with its mysteries and shadows, would be their refuge for the night— an unexpected stop on their journey, but one that added just the right amount of excitement and curiosity to their adventure.

Alone in the dimly lit chamber, Siya's nerves were on edge as she stepped into the shower. The room was suffused with an eerie silence, broken only by the steady drip of water from the faucet. As Siya stepped into the shower, the warm water cascading over her, she let out a sigh of relief. The fatigue from the long drive began to melt away, and for a moment, everything seemed peaceful. The soft sound of water hitting the tiles was almost hypnotic. But then, something shifted. The warm steam that had enveloped her started to dissipate unnaturally fast, replaced by a sharp chill that made her skin prickle. And, as she lathered soap onto her skin, a rapid revolution in temperature sent a shiver down her spine. She paused, suddenly aware of the eerie silence outside the bathroom, her heart rate increasing.

The air felt heavy, like something was pressing in around her. The temperature dropped further, goosebumps rising on her skin as she reached for the shampoo. A strange, unsettling feeling crept into her chest—like she wasn't alone. The shadows in the corners of the room seemed to stretch, and the faintest rustle of movement outside the shower curtain made her stop mid-motion. Siya's breath hitched as she stood frozen, the sound of water splashing in the silence feeling unnervingly loud.

A cold draft swept past her, making the shower curtain flutter slightly, almost like something—or someone—had brushed past it. Her heart pounded harder in her chest. "It's nothing... it's just my mind playing tricks," she whispered to herself, but her body didn't believe it. Every instinct screamed that something was wrong. She felt eyes on her, a presence lurking just beyond the thin barrier of the curtain. The air grew thick and oppressive, and Siya felt as though she was being watched, unseen eyes boring into her from the darkness beyond. Unable to ignore it any longer, Siya, trembling with fear and anticipation, gripped the edge of the curtain, willing herself to be brave. The sensation of being watched grew unbearable, like cold fingers trailing down her spine. Taking a deep breath, with a trembling hand she yanked the curtain back, with dreadfilled anticipation her heart pounding in her ears.

To her horror, there was nothing there—no one hiding in the shadows, no explanation for the chilling sensation that had enveloped her. Nothing.

The bathroom was empty. The only sound was the water still hitting the tiles, and yet, the dread didn't leave her. She was alone, but the feeling of being watched hadn't gone away. But as she turned back her gaze flicked to the mirror above the sink, and her blood ran cold. There, in the foggedup mirror, was the clear imprint of a hand—large, dripping wet, as if someone had been standing right in front of it just moments ago. But the door was still locked. No one could have entered.

Her throat tightened, and she backed up, her foot slipping slightly on the wet floor. Panic rose in her chest, her heart hammering against her ribs. The handprint seemed to pulse, almost like it was pressing through the glass, and as she stared, the temperature in the room plummeted even further.

Her breath fogged up in front of her, the moisture in the air freezing. She could hear her own heartbeat thudding loudly, a rush of adrenaline coursing through her veins. Then, without warning, the lights flickered and went out, plunging the room into near darkness. Only the faint glow from the moon outside filtered through the tiny bathroom window, casting eerie shadows on the wall.

Siya stood there, paralyzed by fear, her body too cold and her mind too frantic to react. Her eyes remained glued to the mirror, terrified that if she looked away, something—someone—might appear. The silence was deafening, only the dripping of water echoing in the suffocating stillness. Slowly, with shaking hands, she reached for the towel, wrapping it around herself, her movements quick and desperate.

And then she heard it—a faint, almost imperceptible whisper. A cold breath against her ear, though no one was there. "You're not alone..."

Siya gasped, turning around frantically, but the bathroom was as empty as it had been. The handprint on the mirror, however, had not faded.

As Kabir entered the room, Siya rushed toward him, her face pale and her eyes wide with fear. She told him about the handprint on the mirror, the chilling sensation in the bathroom, and the strange whisper that had made her skin crawl. Kabir, though skeptical at first, could feel an unnatural heaviness in the air around them—something dark, something oppressive. His eyes darted to the shadows lingering in the corners, unnervingly still yet filled with an eerie presence.

They both stood in the middle of the room, scanning every corner. Kabir could sense the shift in the atmosphere, the coldness wrapping around them like an unwelcome guest. The decision to stay seemed logical in the face of the hour—they had already spent money on the booking, and it was too late to leave. But deep down, they both knew they had no choice but to face the night together.

"Let's try to get some sleep," Kabir suggested, though neither of them truly believed rest would come easily.

They lay down, the bed cold beneath them despite the blankets. Meanwhile, Kabir's unease grew as he sensed a malevolent presence lurking in the glooms. The darkness in the room seemed thicker than usual, pressing in from all sides. Kabir could feel Siya's hand tremble in his, and he squeezed it reassuringly, but his own nerves were frayed. He could barely close his eyes, his senses hyper-aware of every sound, every shift in the shadows.

Hours seemed to stretch painfully. Siya huddled in the corner of the bed, her eyes wide with fear, as shadowy figures danced in the periphery of her vision. Each creak of the floorboards and rustle of the curtains sent her heart racing, her mind consumed by the terror of the unknown. At some point, Kabir drifted off, but it wasn't long before he woke with a start. He felt it—a pressure on his chest, heavy and suffocating, as if something was pinning him down. His breath hitched, and when he tried to move, he found himself paralyzed, unable to even call out to Siya. Panic surged through him. In the corner of his eye, he saw a figure—a dark, shadowy silhouette standing at the edge of the room, watching him. Panic surged through him as he struggled to draw air into his lungs, the sensation of suffocation tightening its grip.

His heart raced, his mind screaming for him to move, but he was trapped in place, helpless under the heap of whatever was holding him down. Cold sweat drenched his body, and his pulse thundered in his ears. He felt the figure inch closer, the stench of decay filling the air, thick and nauseating. Just as he was about to give in to terror, he let out a guttural, desperate shout, wrenching himself free from the grip of the invisible force.

Siya bolted upright, startled by his scream. "What happened?" she asked, her voice quivering. Siya, startled by

Kabir's gasps for air, reached out to him in the darkness, her fingers trembling with fear. Together, they clung to each other. Kabir panted, his body shaking as he struggled to find his words. "Something... something was holding me down. I couldn't move." He wiped the sweat from his forehead, his eyes wide and frantic. "There's something in this room, Siya."

Siya's face turned even paler, her fear mirroring his. "We can't stay here, Kabir. We have to do something."

They scrambled to light the few candles they had packed, but as the night wore on, eerie whispers echoed through the room, their words chilling to the bone. Their flickering flames casting dancing shadows on the walls. The shadows seemed to shift, morphing into shapes that lurked in the corners, waiting, watching. The temperature in the room had dropped so low they could see their breath. Every creak, every whisper of wind outside made their hearts race faster.

"We need to pray," Kabir whispered, his voice shaking. "It's the only thing we can do."

Holding hands, they began to recite prayers, their voices trembling but steadying with each word. The darkness seemed to press harder around them, but they kept going, pouring every ounce of faith they had into their words. The stench of decay lingered, and they could feel the oppressive presence in the room, but the prayers became their lifeline, a beacon of hope in the suffocating darkness.

Time passed excruciatingly slowly. Every moment felt like an eternity as they huddled together, their eyes flicking to the dark corners where the shadows twisted unnaturally. The curtains swayed lightly despite the absence of wind, and the faintest whisper of movement could be heard beneath their prayers. But neither Kabir nor Siya stopped reciting, their faith unwavering in the face of terror.

Siya felt the touch of cold fingers brushing against her arm once, but she didn't flinch. She clung to Kabir, her prayers becoming louder, more fervent. Kabir, too, felt the presence closing in, a breath on the back of his neck, but he refused to acknowledge it, focusing only on the rhythm of their words.

The night stretched on, tormenting them with its relentless darkness. But just as they thought they could bear no more, the first hint of dawn broke through the window—a faint, silvery light that seemed to pierce through the thick gloom in the room. As the sunlight began to filter in, the fear in the air lifted. The shadows receded, and the stench slowly dissipated.

Kabir and Siya exchanged a look, exhausted but relieved. Without a word, they gathered their belongings, leaving the room as soon as the light was strong enough to guide them. Neither of them looked back as they closed the door behind them.

The night had been a trial—one of fear, darkness, and faith. But in the end, it was their prayers, and their trust in each other, that had carried them through the night.

As the first rays of dawn pierced through the thick curtains, Kabir and Siya, exhausted but filled with relief, wasted no time. They quickly packed their belongings, hearts racing, as they fled the haunted inn. The eerie chill of the night still clung to them, but the warmth of the sun brought a sense of hope. Their souls bore the scars of the horrors they had witnessed— whispers in the shadows, ghostly handprints on the mirror, and the suffocating stench that had haunted them through the night. But now, with the light of day, they felt free.

They jumped into their car, driving away as fast as they could, leaving the cursed inn behind. Neither of them spoke for a while, too shaken to revisit the horrors just yet. But as the road stretched out before them, winding through peaceful countryside, the tension slowly began to lift. The sun climbed higher, the trees swayed in the gentle breeze, and soon enough, they found themselves laughing at their misfortune, realizing that they had survived.

The rest of the trip was a stark contrast to the harrowing night they had endured. After a quick pit stop for breakfast, where they indulged in hot coffee and freshly baked pastries, their spirits lifted. The drive ahead took them through stunning landscapes—rolling hills, lush valleys, and crystal-clear rivers that shimmered in the sunlight.

Siya, as usual, took charge of the music, curating the perfect road trip playlist that had them both singing along. They stopped at a quaint little village, where they explored local shops, tried out traditional snacks, and even bought each other silly souvenirs.

As the trip went on, the bond between them grew stronger. They shared funny anecdotes from their pasts, making each other laugh till their sides hurt. Kabir playfully teased Siya about her dancing in front of the mirror while getting ready, and she jokingly called him out for always being late. There were maddening moments too—like when Kabir missed a turn and got them lost for a while, but even that added to the fun as they navigated back, guided by laughter and adventure.

By the time they reached their final destination, they were no longer haunted by the nightmares of the inn. The horrors of that night had been replaced with joy, laughter, and unforgettable memories. The rest of the trip was a celebration of life, resilience, and the strength of their friendship, proving that no matter what darkness they might face, they could always find light in each other's company.

In this chapter, Kabir and Siya face an overwhelming and terrifying experience, surrounded by darkness and the unsettling presence of something beyond the natural. Despite their fear and the unknown forces against them, they find strength in their faith. Together, they turn to prayer, holding onto each other and trusting in the power of their beliefs. Their unwavering faith becomes their shield, pushing back the fear and darkness. The message here is clear: no matter how strong the challenges or how terrifying the situation, faith and trust in God can provide light even in the darkest of times, reminding us that no evil can truly defeat the power of belief.

Chapter 10
The Night the Stars Fell

Amidst the post-glow of their countryside adventure, Kabir and Siya often found themselves reminiscing about the unforgettable moments they had shared. The laughter, the joy, and the simple pleasures of discovering new places together were memories they cherished deeply. They remembered the sunlit roads stretching out before them, the fresh air that seemed to carry away all their worries, and the playful conversations that filled the spaces between the scenic views. Every twist and turn of the journey seemed to bring them closer, weaving a tapestry of shared experiences that they knew would last a lifetime.

But even as they recalled the laughter and excitement, a shiver would sometimes run down their spines when they thought about the first night at the haunted inn. That night, with its suffocating darkness and chilling presence, had left an indelible mark on them both. The cold shadows, the inexplicable noises, the eerie sensation of being watched—it was an experience that had shaken them to their core. They could still feel the dread that had seeped into their bones, the way their hearts had pounded in fear, and the sense of relief that had flooded them when the first light of dawn had finally broken through.

The Amaranthine Promises: Where love finds its way in the labyrinth of fate, illuminating the path to redemption and renewal. With each page turned, you may find solace in the power of forgiveness and boundless depths of true love.

Despite the horror of that night, what stood out even more vividly were the happy moments that followed. There was the thrill of the open road, the spontaneity of their pit stops, and the sheer joy of being in each other's company. They laughed until their sides ached over silly jokes, shared secrets under the starlit sky, and felt the freedom of the countryside as they explored hidden trails and discovered breath-taking views.

It was these moments that defined their trip—the unplanned detours, the shared meals at roadside stalls, the music that played softly in the background as they drove through the quiet, winding roads. Every smile, every shared glance, and every carefree moment seemed to erase the shadows of that haunted night, replacing them with the warmth of companionship and the excitement of adventure. But amidst the tales of sun-soaked beaches and lively nightlife, one incident stood out as particularly memorable – the infamous bike mishap at the club.

It all started innocently enough. Kabir and Siya had decided to let loose and celebrate their growing closeness with a night out at one of the city's most popular clubs, "Pulse 21". As they stepped into the vibrant, pulsating atmosphere, they were greeted by a sea of flashing lights, throbbing music, and the heady mix of laughter and chatter that filled the air.

Siya looked radiant in a knee-length, off-shoulder black dress that hugged her curves perfectly, shimmering slightly under the club lights. Her hair, cascading in loose waves over her shoulders, framed her glowing face. She wore a subtle shade of red lipstick that complemented her dark eyes, which sparkled with excitement and anticipation. Kabir couldn't help but steal glances at her every now and then, his heart skipping a beat at how stunning she looked.

Kabir, on the other hand, had opted for a casual yet sophisticated look. He wore a crisp white shirt, its sleeves rolled up just below the elbow, paired with dark denim jeans. His neatly groomed beard and tousled hair added an edge to his otherwise clean look. A simple silver watch gleamed on his wrist, completing his effortlessly cool style. As they made their way to the bar, Siya playfully tugged at his sleeve, leaning in close to be heard over the music.

"Looking sharp, Mr. Kabir. You clean up well!" she teased with a wink.

"And you, Miss Siya, look absolutely stunning," he replied, a smile lighting up his face. "Are you trying to make all the men in this club jealous tonight?"

Siya laughed, her laughter mixing with the club's upbeat tempo. "Just one man, actually."

The club itself was a sight to behold. It was sprawled across two levels, with a massive dance floor in the centre surrounded by plush seating areas. The DJ booth was elevated, glowing under neon lights as the DJ worked his magic, spinning tracks that kept the crowd moving. Chandeliers hung from the high ceiling, casting a dim, sultry glow over the entire place, while the walls were lined with mirrors, amplifying the sense of space and light. The bar, with its gleaming marble countertop and rows of colourful bottles, was a hub of activity as bartenders skilfully mixed cocktails, their movements a blur of precision and flair.

As the night wore on, the drinks flowed freely, loosening the inhibitions of everyone present. The music pounded, a heady mix of EDM and classic hits that kept the dance floor alive. Kabir, normally reserved, found himself swept up in the exuberance of the night. With each drink, his laughter grew louder, his movements more animated. He danced with Siya, twirling her around with a carefree abandon that made her laugh out loud.

"Who knew you could dance like this?" she teased, her eyes shining as they moved to the rhythm.

Kabir shrugged, a wide grin spreading across his face. "There's a lot you don't know about me yet."

"Is that so?" Siya leaned in closer, her voice playful. "What else are you hiding, Mr. Mysterious?"

"Guess you'll have to stick around to find out," he shot back, his voice dropping to a conspiratorial whisper.

As the night wore on, Kabir's exuberance got the best of him. The alcohol coursing through his veins made him bolder, more reckless. He started dancing on the bar, much to the amusement and cheers of the crowd around them. Siya watched, half-amused, half-concerned, as he mimicked the DJ's moves, his arms raised in the air, spinning and stumbling slightly.

"Kabir, get down from there!" she called out, trying to keep her voice steady despite her laughter.

The Amaranthine Promises: Where love finds its way in the labyrinth of fate, illuminating the path to redemption and renewal. With each page turned, you may find solace in the power of forgiveness and boundless depths of true love.

But Kabir was in his element, his usual self-control replaced by a sense of unbridled freedom. "Come on, Siya! Live a little!" he shouted back, his eyes bright with excitement.

The club erupted into applause and cheers, people egging him on as he jumped down, pulling Siya onto the dance floor with him. They moved together, their laughter mingling with the music, their bodies swaying in unison. It felt like they were in their own world, the rest of the club fading into the background as they lost themselves in the moment.

But as the night progressed, Siya could see the signs—Kabir's movements becoming sloppier, his laughter tinged with an edge of something more. She knew she had to step in before things got out of hand. Gently, she pulled him aside, away from the crowd and the blaring music.

"Hey, let's take a break, okay? You've had enough," she said softly, her hand resting on his arm.

Kabir looked at her, his eyes slightly unfocused but filled with affection. "Siya, you're the best," he slurred, leaning closer. "You know that, right?"

She smiled, brushing a stray lock of hair from his forehead. "I know. And you're pretty great too. But let's get some air, yeah?"

With a nod, he let her lead him outside, the cool night air hitting them as they stepped out of the club. The contrast from the loud, crowded space inside to the quiet, calm outside was stark, and it seemed to sober Kabir up slightly. They stood there for a moment, Siya's arm around his waist, as they caught their breath.

"Thanks for looking out for me," Kabir mumbled, his head resting on her shoulder.

"Anytime," she replied, her voice gentle. "But you owe me a dance when you're back to your senses."

He laughed softly, his grip tightening around her. "Deal."

As the cool night breeze hit them outside the club, Kabir's mind buzzed with excitement. He felt invincible, a concoction of adrenaline and alcohol coursing through his veins. Siya, still chuckling from the wild night they had inside, was holding onto his arm, trying to steer him toward their parked bike. She knew he was tipsy, but there was something endearing about his current state—a playful, carefree Kabir that she rarely got to see.

"Come on, Mr. Mysterious," she teased, pulling him gently. "Let's get you back to the hotel before you decide to join the DJ booth again."

Kabir glanced at her, a mischievous glint in his eyes. "Siya, do you trust me?" In a moment of misplaced bravado, he decided to impress Siya with a daring stunt on his rented bike, convinced that he could pull off a move straight out of an action movie.

Siya paused, raising an eyebrow. "I'm starting to question that right now," she joked. "Why?"

Kabir leaned closer, lowering his voice as if revealing a grand secret. "Because I'm about to show you the most epic bike stunt of your life!" He pointed dramatically to his old, yet reliable bike parked nearby. It wasn't exactly a sports bike—more like a modest cruiser that had seen better days—but Kabir was determined to make it his stunt machine for the night.

Siya burst out laughing, shaking her head. "Kabir, are you crazy? You've had too much to drink! Let's just go back."

But Kabir was already striding towards the bike, excitement bubbling over. "Just one stunt, Siya. I promise. You'll love it!" He gave her a wink and mounted the bike, revving the engine, which sputtered and roared to life with a sound more fitting for a lawnmower than a stunt bike.

"Watch this!" he shouted over the noise, grinning widely as Siya stood back, her laughter turning into a mix of amusement and concern. Kabir, clearly overestimating both his skill and the capabilities of the bike, revved the engine a few more times, drawing curious glances from the few remaining patrons outside the club.

With one last dramatic rev, he twisted the throttle and shot forward. The bike lurched, nearly throwing him off balance right from the start. Kabir's eyes widened as he tried to regain control, his grand plan unravelling faster than he could react. The front wheel lifted off the ground—a weak attempt at a wheelie—but instead of smoothly gliding down the street like he had envisioned, the bike wobbled violently.

"Kabir, look out!" Siya shouted, her hands flying to her mouth as Kabir struggled to maintain control.

Before he could fully comprehend what was happening, the bike veered off course, heading straight for a line of parked scooters and bikes. With a resounding crash, Kabir plowed

The Amaranthine Promises: Where love finds its way in the labyrinth of fate, illuminating the path to redemption and renewal. With each page turned, you may find solace in the power of forgiveness and boundless depths of true love.

into the vehicles, toppling them like a row of dominoes. The sound of metal against metal echoed through the street as he was thrown off the bike, landing in an undignified heap on the pavement.

Siya, torn between shock and hilarity, finally gave in and doubled over with laughter. "Oh my god, Kabir! What did you just do?!" she managed to gasp out, tears of laughter streaming down her face.

Kabir, groaning, tried to sit up, his heroic stunt now reduced to a ridiculous, comical failure. He looked up at Siya, who was still laughing uncontrollably, and couldn't help but chuckle himself. "That… didn't go exactly as planned," he muttered sheepishly, rubbing his aching shoulder.

But their amusement was short-lived as a group of burly men, clearly owners of the now-damaged bikes, emerged from the club, their expressions ranging from confusion to anger as they surveyed the chaos. One particularly large man with a thick mustache pointed at Kabir. "Oi! Is that your doing?" he bellowed, his voice loud enough to make Siya stop laughing instantly.

Kabir's eyes widened in panic. "Uh-oh… Time to go!" he whispered frantically to Siya, who nodded, her face suddenly serious.

Without wasting another second, Kabir scrambled to his feet, fumbling with his bike, which, miraculously, still seemed capable of functioning despite the crash. The mob of angry men began advancing, shouting threats and curses.

Kabir, still a bit unsteady, managed to get the bike upright and revved the engine once more. "Get on!" he yelled, and Siya didn't need to be told twice. She hopped on behind him, clutching his waist as the angry voices grew louder.

With a final, desperate twist of the throttle, the bike roared to life and shot forward, the mob mere feet away now. Kabir, adrenaline pumping, swerved around the fallen scooters and sped down the street, Siya holding on tightly, her laughter and fear blending into one.

"Faster, Kabir! They're right behind us!" she shouted, glancing back at the group of men who had now taken to their own bikes, giving chase.

Kabir pushed the bike to its limits, weaving through the narrow streets, his heart pounding in his chest. "I thought they'd be more understanding!" he joked, despite the situation.

"Understanding?! You just crashed into their bikes!" Siya shot back, half laughing, half terrified.

They zipped through the streets, the wind whipping through their hair as the angry shouts of their pursuers faded into the distance. Finally, after what felt like an eternity, they reached a quieter, more deserted part of town. Kabir slowed the bike, breathing heavily, and pulled over, both of them gasping for breath.

As they sat there, the absurdity of the situation hit them, and they both burst out laughing, the sound echoing in the still night air. Siya, still clutching Kabir's back, shook her head in disbelief.

The Amaranthine Promises: Where love finds its way in the labyrinth of fate, illuminating the path to redemption and renewal. With each page turned, you may find solace in the power of forgiveness and boundless depths of true love.

"You are insane, Kabir. Absolutely insane," she said between fits of laughter.

Kabir grinned, turning his head slightly to look at her. "But you've got to admit, that was one hell of a stunt."

Siya swatted his shoulder playfully. "Yeah, a disaster of a stunt!"

As they made their hasty retreat from the scene of the accident, Kabir's heart raced with adrenaline as he dodged the angry shouts and threatening gestures of the bike owners. With Siya by his side, they made a daring escape, ducking and weaving through the crowd with the finesse of seasoned fugitives. They knew this was a night they would never forget—a chaotic, reckless adventure that, in its own way, had brought them closer than ever.

And as they finally reached the safety of the Hotel outside, breathless and exhilarated, Kabir couldn't help but marvel at the absurdity of it all. It was a moment they would never forget, a testament to the unpredictable nature of life and the joy that could be found in even the most unexpected of circumstances.

In the dimly lit hotel room, the adrenaline from their wild escape still pulsed through their veins, a heady mix of fear, excitement, and raw emotion. The moonlight streamed in through the curtains, casting a soft glow over the room making everything appear surreal and dreamlike. Kabir and Siya stood by the window their breath still coming in short bursts, a lingering reminder of the chaos they had just unfolded.

They looked at each other, their eyes locking in an unspoken understanding. The laughter that had once filled the room had faded, replaced by a charged silence, thick with anticipation. Kabir took a step closer, his gaze never leaving hers. His hand reached out, almost hesitant, brushing a stray lock of hair off from her face. A simple touch sent a jolt of electricity through both of them, igniting something deeper and more primal.

"Siya…" Kabir's voice was a whisper, low and husky, his eyes dark with desire. He could feel the pull between them, A magnetic force drawing him in, demanding he close the distance.

Siya's heart pounded in her chest, her pulse a rapid beat that echoed in her ears. She could feel the heat radiating from him, her skin tingling in response. "Kabir," she breathed, her voice trembling with the same need that she saw reflected in his eyes. There was something intoxicating about the way he looked at her, like she was the only thing that mattered.

Slowly, almost as if testing the boundaries, Kabir leaned in, his face inches from hers. He could feel her breath, warm and unstable mingling, with his. His hand moved to the small of her back, pulling her closer there was barely any space between them. He could feel her softness against his chest, her body trembling slightly, and it took all of his self-control not to lose himself in the moment.

Their lips hovered, just a whisper apart, the tension between them almost unbreakable. Kabir hesitated for a fraction of a second, searching her eyes for a sign of hesitation.

But all he saw was desire, raw and unfiltered, burning in those deep expressive eyes. And then finally he closed the distance, capturing her lips in a kiss that was both gentle and demanding.

It was like a spark had been ignited, a flame that quickly grew into an inferno. Siya responded instantly, her hands sliding up to his shoulders, gripping him as if afraid he might disappear. The Kiss deepened, their lips moving together with an urgency that surprised them both. It was as if every unspoken word, every hidden feeling they had been holding back, was pouring out in that single, searing kiss.

Kabir's hand just roamed over her back, exploring caressing, his touch sending shivers down her spine. Siya melted into him, her body arching instinctively, pressing closer as if trying to erase last vestiges of space between them. The kiss grew more fervent, more desperate, their tongues dancing in a rhythm that felt as old as time itself. It was kiss that spoke of need and longing, of passion that had been simmering beneath, waiting for the right moment to explode.

They stumbled back, Kabir's legs hitting the edge of the bed. He broke the kiss for a brief moment, his forehead resting against hers, both of them breathing heavily, their hearts racing. "Siya, I –" he started but, she silenced him with another kiss, her fingers threading through his hair, tugging him closer.

"I know Kabir," she whispered against his lips, her voice barely more than a breathless murmur. "I know."

With a low growl, Kabir wrapped his arms around her, lifting her effortlessly as he turned and laid her down on the bed. He hovered above her, his eyes raking over her face, memorizing every detail, every curve and line. She looked up at him, her hair fanned out on the pillow, her lips swollen from their kisses, her eyes dark and inviting. She was beautiful, more beautiful than he had ever dared to imagine, and it took his breath away.

Siya reached up, her fingers trailing over his jaw, down his neck, feeling the hard lines of his muscles beneath his shirt. "Kabir…" she whispered, and that single word, said with so much emotion, broke whatever restraint he had left.

He dipped hi head, his lips trailing over her jaw, down the column of her neck, tasting her savoring the soft sighs that escaped her lips. His hands roamed over her body, feeling the warmth of her skin beneath the thin fabric of her dress. She arched against him, her hands clutching his shoulders, pulling him closer, her body trembling with anticipation.

Their clothes were blurred, discarded carelessly as they explored each other, touch by touch, kiss by kiss. Every caress, every whispered word, was filled with the hunger that neither of them had known existed. The world outside faded away, leaving just the two of them, lost in each other, lost in the heat and passion that burned between them.

As Kabir's lips met hers again, the kiss was different this time-slow, deep, filled with tenderness that made her heart ache. The bodies moved together in perfect harmony, a dance, a Symphony of desire and need. They surrendered to the moment, to the raw, primal urge that had brought them together, the movies growing more urgent, more desperate.

The Amaranthine Promises: Where love finds its way in the labyrinth of fate, illuminating the path to redemption and renewal. With each page turned, you may find solace in the power of forgiveness and boundless depths of true love.

Siya clung to him, her nails digging into his back as he drove her higher, pushed her closer to the edge. The air was thick with the scent of them, of their passion, their mingled breaths, the only sound in the room. And when we finally tumbled over the edge, it was like the world shattered around them, leaving them breathless, trembling, and utterly consumed by the force of their love.

They lay there, wrapped in each other's arms, their hearts still racing, their bodies tangled together. Kabir pressed a soft kiss to her forehead, his hand brushing back the hair from her face as he looked down at her with tenderness that made her chest tighten.

"Siya," he whispered, his voice filled with wonder and awe. "I don't know what this is, but I know I don't want it to end."

Siya smiled, her fingers tracing the contours of his face, memorizing every line, and shadow. "Neither do I, Kabir. Neither do I."

In the quiet hours before dawn, as they lay entwined in each other's embrace, Kabir and Siya knew that they had shared something truly special. It was a moment of pure and unbridled intimacy, a testament to the depth of their connection and the power of their love.

And as they drifted off to sleep, their hearts still racing with the memory of their passion, Kabir and Siya knew that their journey together was just beginning. For in each other's arms, they had found a love that was as boundless as the ocean and as timeless as the stars.

The Amaranthine Promises: Where love finds its way in the labyrinth of fate, illuminating the path to redemption and renewal. With each page turned, you may find solace in the power of forgiveness and boundless depths of true love.

In a moment of divine serenity, Kabir and Siya find themselves bathed in the celestial glow of a meteor shower, their hearts united in a symphony of love and longing. As they gaze up at the heavens above, they are reminded of the infinite possibilities that lie ahead, guided by the light of their shared destiny.

The Amaranthine Promises: Where love finds its way in the labyrinth of fate, illuminating the path to redemption and renewal. With each page turned, you may find solace in the power of forgiveness and boundless depths of true love.

Chapter 11
Bridges of Forgiveness

As the sun rose over the horizon, casting a golden glow over the city streets, Kabir and Siya awoke to a new day filled with endless possibilities. As they settled back into their daily routines, a cloud of tension began to loom over their relationship. For Kabir, the sting of disappointment gnawed at him as he learned of Siya's recent promotion at work. Despite his efforts, he had not received the same recognition, and a seed of resentment began to take root in his heart.

It was a quiet evening at a cozy restaurant, the soft glow of candlelight casting shadows on the table where Kabir and Siya sat. The atmosphere felt heavy, laden with unspoken words and simmering resentment. Kabir's eyes, usually warm and full of affection, were distant, clouded by frustration and disappointment. Siya, sensing his unease, tried to lighten the mood.

Siya: "You know, I was thinking we could take a short trip this weekend. Just get away from everything, clear our heads. What do you think?"

Kabir stirred his drink absently, his gaze fixed on the swirling liquid.

Kabir: "Yeah, that sounds nice," he said flatly, the enthusiasm that usually accompanied his words conspicuously absent.

Siya frowned, leaning forward slightly. "Kabir, what's wrong? You've been so distant lately."

He sighed deeply, finally looking up at her, the irritation barely concealed in his eyes. "Nothing's wrong, Siya. Just... life, I guess."

Siya reached out to touch his hand, but he pulled away subtly, his body language closing off. "Is it about the promotion?" she asked softly, her voice laced with concern.

Kabir let out a bitter laugh. "Oh, so you did notice," he said sarcastically, his eyes narrowing slightly. "Congrats on yours, by the way. I guess it's easier when... you know."

Siya blinked, taken aback. "Easier when what, Kabir?"

Kabir's expression hardened, his frustration boiling over. "When you're beautiful, Siya. When you're a woman," he spat out, his voice dripping with bitterness. "You think I didn't see how they fawn over you, how they bend over backwards to make things easier for you?"

Siya recoiled as if she'd been slapped, her eyes widening in shock. "Are you seriously saying that my promotion was because of my looks and gender?" she whispered, her voice shaking with a mix of anger and hurt.

Kabir didn't back down. "Well, isn't it true?" he retorted, his words harsh and cutting. "You don't have to fight for everything like I do. One smile, one flirtatious laugh, and doors just open for you."

Tears welled up in Siya's eyes, but she blinked them away, her expression turning cold. "How dare you, Kabir? How can you reduce everything I've worked for, all the late nights, the hard work, to just my looks?"

Kabir's face twisted in anger. "You don't get it, Siya. You have no idea how it feels to be constantly overlooked, to work your ass off and still be told you're not good enough. And then watch someone else—someone you love—just sail through as if it's nothing."

Siya's hands trembled as she clenched them into fists on the table. "You think it's been easy for me?" she said, her voice low but fierce. "You think I haven't had to prove myself, fight off inappropriate comments and unwanted advances, just to be taken seriously? You think my success is because of my gender?"

Kabir looked away, his jaw clenched, the impact of his words hanging heavily between them.

Siya: "You're being unfair, Kabir," she continued, her voice cracking with emotion. "I've supported you through everything. And now you throw this at me? Do you even realize how hurtful that is?"

He rubbed his temples, suddenly feeling ashamed but still unable to swallow his pride. "Maybe I am being unfair. But it's hard, Siya. Watching you succeed while I'm stuck. It's... humiliating."

The Amaranthine Promises: Where love finds its way in the labyrinth of fate, illuminating the path to redemption and renewal. With each page turned, you may find solace in the power of forgiveness and boundless depths of true love.

Siya took a deep breath, straightening her back. She looked directly into his eyes, her voice unwavering. "I'm sorry you feel that way, but you don't get to belittle my achievements because you're going through a rough patch," she said, her tone firm and resolute. "I've earned this promotion, Kabir, and I won't let anyone—least of all you—diminish it."

Kabir was taken aback by the steel in her voice. This wasn't the Siya who would shrink back from confrontation, who would let things slide to keep the peace. This was a side of her he hadn't seen before—uncompromising and unyielding.

"I've always believed in you," she continued, her eyes blazing with intensity. "But I won't allow you to disrespect me like this. If you can't support me, if you can't be happy for me, then we have a bigger problem than just a promotion."

Kabir felt a pang of guilt as he watched her, the realization of how deeply his words had cut dawning on him. "I'm sorry, Siya," he murmured, his voice barely audible. "I didn't mean it."

Siya held his gaze, unflinching. "You did, Kabir. And it's something I'll remember. I'm willing to work through this, but you need to get past your insecurities. I won't be your punching bag whenever things don't go your way.

The conviction in her words left him speechless. He knew he had crossed a line, one that might not be easy to come back from. The rest of the evening passed in strained silence, each lost in their own turmoil, the chasm between them widening with every passing second.

The Amaranthine Promises: Where love finds its way in the labyrinth of fate, illuminating the path to redemption and renewal. With each page turned, you may find solace in the power of forgiveness and boundless depths of true love.

As the days turned into weeks, the tension between Kabir and Siya simmered beneath the surface, lingering like a dark cloud over their relationship. Conversations became strained, and the silence between them was filled with unspoken words, growing heavier with each passing moment. It was as if they were on a precipice, teetering on the edge of an abyss, both too stubborn to take a step back and too afraid to move forward.

So, when an opportunity arose for Kabir to fly to London for work, he seized it eagerly. The prospect of escaping the suffocating atmosphere between them seemed like a breath of fresh air. He convinced himself that the distance would help him clear his head, that time apart would somehow mend the cracks that had begun to form between them. But deep down, he knew he was running—running from his own insecurities, his own inadequacies, and the fear that he was no longer enough for Siya.

London welcomed him with open arms, its vibrant energy a stark contrast to the turmoil he had left behind. Kabir threw himself into the city's whirlwind of activity, drowning his confusion and guilt in its bustling streets and neon-lit nights. The lively pubs, the crowded clubs, and the endless stream of new faces offered him the perfect escape. He partied with colleagues, lost himself in the anonymity of the crowd, and revelled in the intoxicating freedom that the city seemed to offer.

The phone calls to Siya, initially frequent, started to dwindle. His messages became shorter, the calls more hurried. He told himself it was the time difference, the hectic schedule, anything to avoid admitting that he was avoiding her. He found solace in the city's distractions—the charming cafés, the vibrant art galleries, the lively nightlife. He explored London with a fervor that left him exhausted, collapsing into bed at odd hours, too tired to call Siya, to reach out and bridge the growing gap between them.

Siya, back home, tried to be understanding. She told herself that he was busy, that he needed this trip. But as the days passed, the silence between them stretched, becoming a chasm she could no longer ignore. She waited for his calls, her heart sinking a little more each time he didn't. His rare messages felt empty, devoid of the warmth and affection that had once been so abundant. It was as if he had left more than just their city behind, he had left her behind too.

She would sit by her phone, hoping it would ring, longing to hear his voice. When it did, her excitement quickly turned to disappointment as their conversations became increasingly superficial. He spoke of his days, the places he visited, the people he met, but never about them, never about what was truly on his mind. She missed the connection they used to have, the way he would listen, truly listen, and the way he made her feel like she was the only one who mattered.

Meanwhile, Kabir lost himself in the lively streets of London. From the iconic landmarks to the hidden gems of the city, he explored it all. The vibrant energy of the city was a stark contrast to the emotions he was running from. Nights blurred into mornings as he drowned his unease in laughter, alcohol, and the thrill of being in a new place. The city, with its relentless pace, made it easy to forget, easy to pretend that everything was fine.

The Amaranthine Promises: Where love finds its way in the labyrinth of fate, illuminating the path to redemption and renewal. With each page turned, you may find solace in the power of forgiveness and boundless depths of true love.

He explored the bustling markets of Camden, wandered through the historic charm of Covent Garden, and lost himself in the electrifying nightlife of Soho. He mingled with strangers, made new acquaintances, and partied with colleagues until the early hours of the morning, his laughter masking the emptiness gnawing at his heart. Every now and then, he would glance at his phone, see Siya's missed calls or her messages, and a fleeting sense of guilt would overwhelm him. But he dismissed it as quickly as it came, convincing himself that he deserved this time, this freedom.

Siya's messages, once a lifeline to him, now felt like an inconvenience, an unwelcome reminder of the life he had momentarily left behind. He told himself he would call her later, knowing full well that 'later' never came. She spent sleepless nights staring at her phone, hoping against hope that it would ring, that he would call and everything would be alright again. But it didn't. She watched his social media updates, saw the photos of him laughing with friends, living a life that seemed so distant from the one they had shared.

She missed him terribly, her heart aching with a longing that consumed her. But more than that, she missed the man he used to be—the one who would call her just to hear her voice, the one who would move mountains just to see her smile. She missed the Kabir who made her feel cherished, who made her feel like they were in this together, no matter what.

And Kabir, in his misguided attempt to escape, failed to see the damage he was causing. He was so consumed by his own need for freedom, his own fear of inadequacy, that he couldn't see how his actions were slowly tearing Siya apart.

The Amaranthine Promises: Where love finds its way in the labyrinth of fate, illuminating the path to redemption and renewal. With each page turned, you may find solace in the power of forgiveness and boundless depths of true love.

He was so caught up in the illusion of his newfound independence that he couldn't see the cracks widening in the foundation of their relationship.

In his mind, he was simply taking a break, enjoying his life, living in the moment. But in reality, he was drifting further and further away from the one person who mattered the most. He was blind to the pain he was causing, deaf to her silent pleas, and numb to the love that was slowly slipping through his fingers.

And so, while Kabir lost himself in the bustling streets of London, Siya was left behind, grappling with the suffocating silence, her heart breaking a little more with each passing day. For every night he spent laughing with strangers, she spent lying awake, wondering where they went wrong, her heart heavy with a loneliness that seemed to have no end.

Amidst the uncertainty of her strained relationship with Kabir, Siya found herself at a crossroads. The late summer evening carried a sense of heaviness, the air thick with unspoken words and unanswered questions. Her mind was a whirlwind of thoughts as she pondered the unexpected proposal that had landed in her lap—a proposal that promised everything she had ever been told she should want.

The man in question was the son of her father's old friend, a well-established businessman who had built a successful life in the picturesque city of Venice. He was everything her parents had hoped for in a match— handsome, educated, stable, and deeply respectful. The prospect of marriage to someone like him brought with it the promise of security, the comfort of a stable life, and the certainty of a future devoid of turmoil. It was a tempting offer, especially in contrast to the chaos that Kabir's absence had left in its wake.

But as Siya sat in her bedroom, staring at the neatly written letter that accompanied the proposal, she couldn't shake the feeling that something was amiss. The man was perfect on paper, his credentials impeccable. Yet, the thought of a life with him felt hollow, devoid of the passion and excitement she craved. It was a life that was carefully curated, planned down to the last detail, but it wasn't her life.

She stood up and walked to the window, looking out at the cityscape that stretched before her. The setting sun bathed everything in a warm, golden hue, casting long shadows that seemed to echo the confusion in her heart. She knew that accepting this proposal would make her parents happy, that it would bring them peace of mind. But what about her own peace of mind? What about her own happiness?

The sound of her father's footsteps broke her reverie. He entered the room quietly, his presence a comforting reminder of the love and support that had always been her anchor.

"Siya," he began gently, his voice tinged with concern. "I know you've been going through a lot lately, and I understand that this proposal has come at a complicated time. But I want you to know that your mother and I only want what's best for you. We don't want you to make any decisions out of pressure or fear."

She turned to look at him, his kind eyes filled with a quiet wisdom that she had always admired. "I know, Papa," she said softly, her voice barely above a whisper. "But I don't know what to do. On one hand, this proposal seems perfect. He's everything you and Mama have ever wanted for me. But on the other hand… it doesn't feel right. It doesn't feel like my life."

Her father nodded, stepping closer to her and taking her hand in his. "I understand. And I want you to know that whatever decision you make, we will support you. But I also want you to think carefully. This young man, he's a good person. He comes from a good family, and he respects you. I've seen how he looks at you, Siya. He's genuinely interested in you as a person, not just in fulfilling some obligation."

Siya felt a pang of guilt at her father's words. She knew he was right. The man had been nothing but kind and respectful, his intentions sincere. But even so, there was a nagging emptiness that she couldn't ignore.

"I know, Papa," she said, her voice trembling slightly. "But I can't just marry someone because they're nice to me. It has to be more than that. It has to be… love, right?"

Her father smiled gently, his eyes softening with a tenderness that made her heart ache. "Yes, my dear, it has to be love. But love is complicated. It's not always fireworks and grand gestures. Sometimes, it's quiet, steady, and reliable. It's someone who stands by you, who respects your dreams and supports your ambitions. It's someone who can offer you stability and a future."

He paused, searching her face for a sign of understanding. "But I also know that you're not ready to settle for something

The Amaranthine Promises: Where love finds its way in the labyrinth of fate, illuminating the path to redemption and renewal. With each page turned, you may find solace in the power of forgiveness and boundless depths of true love.

just because it's comfortable. You're my daughter, after all. You have that same stubborn streak as your mother and me," he added with a chuckle, trying to lighten the mood.

Siya smiled, a tear slipping down her cheek. "Papa, I'm scared. What if I make the wrong choice? What if I let go of something good because I'm holding on to a dream that will never come true?"

Her father squeezed her hand, his gaze unwavering. "The only way to find out is to follow your heart, Siya. But whatever you decide, you need to be sure. Don't rush into anything because of fear or uncertainty. Take your time, and if you feel like you need to talk to Kabir before making a decision, do that."

Siya nodded, her heart heavy with the weight of his words. She knew her father was right. She needed to have one last conversation with Kabir, to understand where they stood before she could even think about making such a life-altering decision.

"Thank you, Papa," she whispered, wrapping her arms around him in a tight hug. "I just want to make you and Mama proud."

"You already do, my darling," he murmured into her hair, his voice thick with emotion. "You already do."

That night, as Siya lay in bed, staring up at the ceiling, she made a silent vow. She would wait for Kabir to return. She would talk to him, lay everything out, and then she would make her decision. It was her life, after all, and she owed it to herself to choose what truly made her happy.

The Amaranthine Promises: Where love finds its way in the labyrinth of fate, illuminating the path to redemption and renewal. With each page turned, you may find solace in the power of forgiveness and boundless depths of true love.

Kabir's last few weeks in London were supposed to be a whirlwind of excitement and achievement. Yet, the euphoria he had once felt was replaced by a deep, aching hollowness that gnawed at him day and night. The city that had initially seemed so vibrant and full of life now felt cold and distant, its charm lost in the emptiness that mirrored the void in his heart. No matter how much he tried to distract himself with work and social events, nothing seemed to fill the gaping chasm left by Siya's absence.

It was a late evening when Kabir finally faced the reality he had been avoiding for weeks. He was alone in his hotel room, the silence almost deafening. The city lights outside flickered like tiny beacons, but they did nothing to lift the darkness within him. He glanced around the room, his eyes landing on the scattered mess of clothes and empty takeaway boxes. It was a stark contrast to the orderly life he had once shared with Siya. He remembered how she used to scold him for leaving his shoes lying around, her playful reprimands always followed by a smile that lit up her entire face.

"God, I miss her," he muttered to himself, his voice breaking the silence.

But missing her wasn't enough, and he knew it. It wasn't enough to simply long for her presence or to wish she were there to fill the emptiness. He had to confront the harsh truth: he was the reason she wasn't. He was the one who had driven her away with his careless words and his thoughtless actions.

Kabir sank down onto the edge of the bed, burying his face in his hands. The guilt was suffocating, wrapping around him like a vise that refused to let go. He replayed the dinner in his mind, the look of hurt in Siya's eyes when he had made that horrible, thoughtless comment about her promotion. It was a look he would never forget, one that haunted him every night.

"What the hell were you thinking, Kabir?" he whispered to himself, his voice laced with self-loathing.

He had been a fool, letting his insecurities and frustrations get the better of him. He had projected his own disappointments onto her, punishing her for something that was never her fault. And now, he was paying the price, alone in a city that felt foreign and unwelcoming without her.

As he sat there, a fierce debate raged within him, his conscience tearing into him with a brutal honesty he had been avoiding.

"You pushed her away, Kabir," the voice in his head accused, cold and relentless. "You had everything you ever wanted, and you threw it away because of your own ego. Do you really think she'll be waiting for you after the way you treated her?"

"I didn't mean to hurt her," he argued back, his voice desperate even in his own mind. "I was just… I was frustrated, okay? I was angry and disappointed, and I took it out on her."

"And that makes it okay?" his conscience retorted, the harshness of its tone cutting through him like a knife. "You think you can just apologize, and everything will be fine? You think a few words will erase the pain you caused her?"

The Amaranthine Promises: Where love finds its way in the labyrinth of fate, illuminating the path to redemption and renewal. With each page turned, you may find solace in the power of forgiveness and boundless depths of true love.

Kabir clenched his fists, his knuckles turning white. "I know I messed up. I know I don't deserve her forgiveness. But I can't just let her go without trying. I need to make this right." The voice softened, just a little, as if sensing his resolve. "Do you even know how to make it right, Kabir? Do you understand what it will take to earn back her trust?"

He thought about it, the gravity of the question settling heavily on his shoulders. He knew it wouldn't be easy. He had shattered something precious between them, something that might never be fully mended. But he also knew that he couldn't live with himself if he didn't try. He loved her, more than he had ever loved anyone, and he was willing to do whatever it took to make things right.

"I'll do anything," he said, his voice firm with determination. "I'll swallow my pride, I'll beg if I have to. I'll show her that I'm willing to change, that I'm willing to be the man she deserves."

"And what if she's moved on?" the voice asked, the question hanging in the air like a dark cloud. For the first time, Kabir realized that if he didn't change, he could lose Siya—not to some promotion or rival, but to his own bitterness and jealousy.

Kabir's heart clenched at the thought, a wave of fear crashing over him. It was a possibility, one he hadn't been brave enough to truly consider. What if she had found someone else? Someone who treated her with the respect and love she deserved? The thought of losing her forever was almost too much to bear.

The Amaranthine Promises: Where love finds its way in the labyrinth of fate, illuminating the path to redemption and renewal. With each page turned, you may find solace in the power of forgiveness and boundless depths of true love.

"Then I'll accept it," he said quietly, his voice shaking with the effort it took to say the words. "If she's happier without me, then I'll let her go. But I have to try. I have to know that I did everything I could to win her back."

For a moment, there was silence, the kind that felt heavy with the weight of his decision. And then, as if giving its grudging approval, the voice in his head spoke again, this time with a note of cautious hope.

"Then go to her, Kabir. Show her that you're not the man who hurt her that night. Show her that you're willing to fight for her, that you're willing to change. But most importantly, show her that you love her, truly and deeply, and that you're willing to do whatever it takes to prove it."

Kabir took a deep breath, his heart racing with the realization of what he had to do. He was scared, terrified even, but he knew he had no choice. He had to face his fears, had to confront the demons that had driven him away from the one person who mattered most.

He stood up, determination coursing through his veins. He would go back to her, he would apologize with every ounce of sincerity he had, and he would fight for her with everything he had left. Because he couldn't imagine his life without her, and he wasn't willing to give up without a fight.

With a resolve that had been missing for far too long, Kabir made a silent promise to himself and to Siya, wherever she was.

"I'm coming back to you, Siya. And I'm going to make this right, no matter what it takes."

And with that, he began to plan his return, his heart filled with a mixture of fear and hope as he prepared to face the woman he loved, ready to lay his heart bare and pray that she would give him one last chance.

As Kabir boarded the flight home, a storm of thoughts churned in his mind. His heart raced with the anxiety of a thousand unsaid words and apologies. He wanted nothing more than to make things right with Siya, to prove to her that his love was genuine, that he respected her beyond measure. He had spent the entire journey rehearsing what he would say, planning how he would show her that he was truly sorry for his neglect, for taking her for granted.

But as soon as he returned, every attempt to reach out to Siya failed. She kept avoiding him, her silence a painful reminder of how deeply he had hurt her. He could see it in her eyes, the heartbreak that he had caused. No matter what gifts he brought her, they seemed to fall flat, mere tokens that could never compensate for the time, love, and respect she had longed for in these past few weeks.

She was no longer the bright, cheerful Siya he knew. Instead, she was guarded, her heart wrapped in the bitterness of broken promises. His gifts, once cherished, now seemed meaningless. All she needed was his presence, his understanding, his time. But he had been too caught up in his own world, too blind to see how much she had needed him. And now, as he stood helplessly watching her drift away, he felt the weight of his mistakes crushing down on him.

Kabir realized that he had not just lost Siya's trust, but also a part of himself that he feared he might never get back. The ache in his chest was unbearable, the guilt suffocating. He wanted to tell her that he was sorry, that he loved her more than anything, that he would do anything to make it right. But the words caught in his throat, and she remained out of reach, her silence a wall he couldn't break through.

He had hurt her deeply, and now he was paying the price. The path to forgiveness seemed endless, and he could only hope that one day she would let him in again. Until then, all he could do was wait, tormented by the love he had failed to protect and the woman he was desperately trying not to lose.

As the day of the team's annual event approached, Kabir was on edge, waiting for the perfect moment to speak to Siya. He had been rehearsing his words, hoping to finally get through to her, to show her how much he truly cared. But Siya, caught between her own emotions, found herself at a crossroads, uncertain of which path to take. She had spent days wrestling with her heart, torn between the love she still felt for Kabir and the pain he had caused her.

When she stepped into the crowded room that night, the sound of laughter and music spurted her, and for the first time in weeks, she felt a sense of clarity. She realized, with startling certainty, that she was exactly where she was meant to be. Tonight, wasn't about Kabir or the turmoil in her heart; it was about reclaiming herself and finding joy again, even if it was just for a few hours.

The Amaranthine Promises: Where love finds its way in the labyrinth of fate, illuminating the path to redemption and renewal. With each page turned, you may find solace in the power of forgiveness and boundless depths of true love.

She looked like a vision from heaven in her beautiful gown, a soft, ethereal glow surrounding her as she moved through the room. Heads turned, and conversations paused as everyone took in her beauty. Her laughter, which had been missing for so long, rang out like music, and for a moment, all eyes were on her, not because of Kabir, but because of the light she radiated.

As Siya made her way to the dance floor, her heel caught the edge of a rug, causing her to stumble forward. Before she could hit the ground, Kabir, with swift reflexes, dashed towards her and caught her by the arm.

"Careful there," he said, his voice soft yet teasing, pulling her back onto her feet.

"I'm fine," she said, her voice steady despite the turmoil inside her. "I don't need your support, Kabir."

His face fell, and she could see the hurt flash across his features. He opened his mouth to say something, but she held up her hand, stopping him.

"Not tonight," she whispered, her eyes pleading with him to understand. "Please, just... not tonight."

Kabir nodded slowly, the words he had been dying to say swallowed back. He took a step back, giving her the space, she so clearly needed. But as he watched her walk away, a part of him knew that this wasn't just about tonight. It was about all the nights he hadn't been there, all the times he had failed to protect her heart.

The Amaranthine Promises: Where love finds its way in the labyrinth of fate, illuminating the path to redemption and renewal. With each page turned, you may find solace in the power of forgiveness and boundless depths of true love.

And as the music played on, the distance between them felt insurmountable, a chasm of pain and regret that no words could bridge.

As the night wore on, the energy at the party hit an all-time high. The team had gathered in a lively circle, laughing, dancing, and letting loose after a long week of work. Siya, standing near the edge of the group, was enjoying herself with a drink in hand, swaying to the music, when suddenly, out of nowhere, Kali, a co-worker who had clearly had one too many drinks, stumbled toward her.

His hair was a mess, his tie loosely hanging around his neck, and his eyes glazed over with the kind of confidence only alcohol could summon. Before she could react, he dramatically dropped to one knee, his arms stretched out in a grand gesture. "Siya!" he slurred, his words slightly tangled. "Dance with me! I promise, I'll sweep you off your feet!"

Siya's eyes widened in shock, her heart racing. She quickly glanced around, hoping someone would swoop in and save her from this awkward, unexpected situation. But the crowd was too busy laughing and cheering, oblivious to her plight. The music thumped on, and there was no easy escape in sight.

She nervously took a step back, but Kali was relentless, still on his knees, wobbling unsteadily. "I... I swear I can dance better than anyone here. Just... just give me a chance!" His persistence, while well-intentioned, made her even more uncomfortable. She was torn between laughing at his absurdity and wanting to flee the scene.

Before Siya could call for help, a hero appeared—though not in the way she had imagined. Out of the corner of her eye, she saw Kabir striding toward them, his face set in determination but with a mischievous glint in his eye. Without a word, he swooped down and, to her absolute surprise, didn't push Kali away. Instead, he wrapped his arm around Kali's shoulders, pulling him up from the floor.

"Hey, Kali, my man! You're dancing with me tonight!" Kabir declared with enthusiasm, completely stealing the show. The entire team burst into laughter, and Siya watched in disbelief as Kabir began to spin Kali around in an exaggerated waltz, their steps completely out of sync but full of comedic flair.

Kali, clearly too intoxicated to protest, followed Kabir's lead, stumbling along but giggling like a child. Kabir's face was serious, his lips pressed into a tight line as if they were performing some highly sophisticated routine, but his eyes twinkled with amusement. "Don't worry, Siya!" Kabir called out in mock seriousness. "I'll take care of him!"

Siya finally let out a breath she didn't realize she was holding, laughing despite herself. The tension that had built up evaporated as she watched Kabir expertly guide Kali away from her, their ridiculous dance steps leaving the rest of the team in hysterics.

The music changed to a slower tune, and Kabir, with perfect comic timing, pulled Kali closer, resting his head dramatically on Kali's shoulder. "You've got the moves, man," he whispered loudly, his voice dripping with mock romance. "I've never danced with someone like you before."

The entire room erupted in laughter, and even Kali, still in a daze, couldn't help but giggle, seemingly unaware of what was happening. Kabir winked at Siya, who by now was laughing so hard she could hardly stand.

Kali, lost in the moment and leaning heavily on Kabir, suddenly turned to him, slurring, "You… you're my best friend, Kabir."

"And you're mine," Kabir replied solemnly, patting him on the back. "Now, let's get you some water before you propose to someone else."

Kabir gently led Kali away from the dance floor, leaving Siya standing there, a mixture of relief and admiration washing over her. She couldn't help but smile, her heart softening as she watched Kabir handle the entire situation with grace, humour, and charm.

Once Kali was safely seated with a glass of water, Kabir returned to Siya, his expression turning from playful to warm. "You okay?" he asked softly, stepping close to her.

She nodded, her cheeks flushed, not from embarrassment anymore but from the growing warmth she felt toward him. "I am now," she admitted, her voice barely above a whisper.

For a moment, they stood there, the noise of the party fading into the background. Siya looked at him, her heart fluttering in a way that was new and unfamiliar. In that ridiculous, chaotic moment, something had shifted between them.

Kabir, gave her a small bow, grinning. "My lady, if you need rescuing again, you know who to call."

Siya couldn't help but laugh, but as she met his eyes, she realized something deeper had happened. In that funny, silly moment, Kabir had managed to melt her heart a little more, proving that no matter how chaotic life got, he'd always be there, dancing her out of danger—one ridiculous waltz at a time.

Kabir, ever the opportunist, saw his moment. The party was winding down, the music still playing but with a more mellow rhythm, and everyone was either too drunk or too lost in their own conversations to notice much. He strolled up to Siya with a playful grin, mimicking the exaggerated stance Kali had taken earlier—arms outstretched, one knee bent in mock sincerity.

"Siya," Kabir began in an overly dramatic voice, "I too must ask... will you do me the honour of this dance?" He held his hand out, his face a mix of mock seriousness and a mischievous smile.

Siya couldn't help it. She burst out laughing, clutching her stomach as the memory of Kali's earlier antics flashed through her mind. "Are you serious, Kabir?" she asked, still giggling, eyes sparkling with amusement.

"As serious as Kali was," Kabir replied, barely keeping a straight face. "But this time, I promise not to collapse on you or propose."

Siya laughed again, shaking her head, but something about the warmth in Kabir's eyes made her pause. There was more behind his playful tone. She hesitated for a second, then with a smile, she placed her hand in his. "Alright, alright. Let's do this."

Kabir's grin widened as he pulled her onto the dance floor. At first, it was all fun and games—they danced in an exaggerated way, mimicking every ridiculous move they could think of. Kabir twirled her around in exaggerated, clumsy spins, both of them laughing so hard they could barely stand straight. The other guests, still lingering at the party, watched and chuckled, amused by their antics.

But slowly, as the night deepened and the music shifted to something softer, something more meaningful, the mood between them began to change. Kabir's movements became slower, more deliberate. His hand rested gently on her waist as they swayed to the rhythm, his other hand intertwined with hers. Siya noticed the shift and her laughter began to fade, replaced by a quiet smile.

The room around them seemed to disappear. The chatter of the remaining guests, the clinking of glasses, and even the dim lighting—all of it faded into the background as they moved together in sync. The atmosphere was suddenly charged with a tenderness that neither of them had anticipated. Kabir's eyes never left hers, and for the first time that night, they weren't joking around.

Siya felt her heartbeat quicken, a rush of emotions flooding her senses—gratitude, relief, and something else she couldn't quite name. She had always known Kabir could make her laugh, could charm his way through any situation, but this... this was different. As they swayed together, she realized how much she had come to rely on him, how much she treasured the way he could turn a simple moment into something unforgettable.

The music slowed, and without a word, Kabir gently pulled her closer. His cheek brushed against hers, his breath warm against her skin. Siya could feel the strength of his arms around her, the steadiness of his presence, and it made her heart swell. The world outside seemed to fall away, leaving just the two of them in this bubble of quiet intimacy. He knew he couldn't let another moment pass without addressing the tension that had been brewing between them for weeks.

Siya's eyes met his, full of questions, and for a moment, Kabir struggled to find the right words. His heart pounded as he gathered the courage to admit what he had been holding back.

"I've been a fool, Siya," he started, his voice low but steady. "I let my ego get the best of me. I was insecure, and instead of being happy for you, I made it about myself. I hurt you... and I'm truly sorry."

Siya's expression softened, though there was still a flicker of hesitation. Kabir could see the pain his words had caused her, but he also saw the understanding in her eyes. He took a deep breath, stepping closer, his hand gently cupping her face.

"I should have celebrated your success, not torn you down," Kabir continued. "I know I messed up, but I promise,

I'll do better. I just want you to know how much you mean to me."

In that quiet moment, without waiting for her reply, Kabir leaned in and pressed his lips gently against her forehead. It wasn't just a kiss—it was an apology, a plea for forgiveness, and a vow to be the man she deserved. The warmth of her skin beneath his lips made his heart ache with the realization of how much he had risked losing.

Siya closed her eyes as Kabir kissed her forehead, feeling the sincerity in his touch. The tenderness of the moment wrapped around them like a blanket, shielding them from everything else. As he pulled back slightly, she could see the regret and love in his eyes.

For the first time in weeks, the wall between them began to crumble. Kabir leaned in closer, his voice soft, barely audible.

"You know, Siya, I think everyone's figured it out by now," he said, a smile playing on his lips.

"Figured what out?" she whispered, though her heart already knew the answer.

"That we're together. That we're meant to be together."

Siya looked up into his eyes, her heart pounding. She hadn't expected this moment, hadn't anticipated the flood of emotions she would feel. But here it was, clear and undeniable. Kabir's gaze was steady, sincere, and in that instant, she knew he meant every word. Siya felt a sense of peace engulfing her, like a warm blanket on a cold winter night. The tension she hadn't even realized she'd been holding onto began to ease,

The Amaranthine Promises: Where love finds its way in the labyrinth of fate, illuminating the path to redemption and renewal. With each page turned, you may find solace in the power of forgiveness and boundless depths of true love.

replaced by a certainty she hadn't felt in a long time. In Kabir's arms, everything felt right.

The world outside could wait. For now, there was just the two of them, moving together in perfect harmony, their hearts finally aligned with the rhythm of the night. And as the music continued to play softly, Kabir and Siya held onto each other, knowing that this was just the beginning of something much bigger than either of them had imagined.

As the dawn breaks on a new day, Kabir and Siya stand on the precipice of forgiveness, ready to bridge the chasm that separates them from the past. And so, with laughter in their hearts and love in their eyes, Kabir and Siya danced into the night, their bond strengthened by both the fun and the challenges they faced. What began as playful banter transformed into a deeper connection, and as the evening drew to a close, one thing was certain—together, they were ready to take on whatever life had in store for them.

The Amaranthine Promises: Where love finds its way in the labyrinth of fate, illuminating the path to redemption and renewal. With each page turned, you may find solace in the power of forgiveness and boundless depths of true love.

Chapter 12
Love's Dazzling Dawn

As the night wound down and the echoes of laughter faded into the stillness of the night, Kabir found himself standing outside the venue with Siya by his side, the glow of the streetlights casting a soft halo around her delicate features. With a silent understanding passing between them, he hailed a cab and helped her inside, his heart heavy with the grief of his past mistakes and the uncertainty of their future.

As the cab pulled away from the curb and they were enveloped in the warm cocoon of darkness, Kabir found himself unable to tear his gaze away from Siya's ethereal beauty, her eyes shining with unshed tears and her lips trembling with unspoken emotion. In that instant, as they sat in silence, the weight of their shared history pressing down upon them, Kabir felt a surge of longing and regret well up inside him, threatening to consume him whole.

The car moved through the quiet streets, a thick silence hung in the air between Kabir and Siya. The city lights outside flickered past, casting faint shadows on their faces. The trees lining the road swayed gently in the cool night breeze, their branches reaching toward the sky as though trying to grasp the stars. The streets were mostly empty now, the hustle of the day having long faded away, leaving behind the soft hum of the car's engine as their only companion.

The Amaranthine Promises: Where love finds its way in the labyrinth of fate, illuminating the path to redemption and renewal. With each page turned, you may find solace in the power of forgiveness and boundless depths of true love.

Kabir sat in the passenger seat, stealing glances at Siya, his mind racing with thoughts and questions, none of which he had the courage to voice. His heart ached with guilt, the weight of his mistakes heavy on his chest.

He saw how she stared ahead, her eyes fixed on the road, but her mind seemed miles away. He wanted to say something, anything to ease the tension, to break the silence, but the words refused to come.

Instead, he let his eyes speak. As he watched her, he noticed the faint tremble in her hands, resting lightly on her lap. Her brows furrowed. The lines of worry etched on her face. She wasn't angry, at least not visibly— but there was something there, something that was harder for him to decipher. It was as if she had a thousand questions, but she too was struggling to find the words to ask them.

Suddenly, as though some unseen force connected their hearts, Siya turned her head ever so slightly, her eyes meeting his, neither of them needed words. The silence between them spoke volumes, the car becoming a vessel for their unspoken conversation. Kabir's gaze was filled with apology, an unspoken plea for forgiveness. He was silently telling her everything he couldn't manage to say out loud—"I'm sorry. I hurt you. I was wrong."

Siya's eyes, on the other hand, were full of questions. She wasn't angry, but there was a deep sadness that he had placed there. She searched his face, looking for answers—"Why? Why did you push me away? Did you ever stop loving me?"

The Amaranthine Promises: Where love finds its way in the labyrinth of fate, illuminating the path to redemption and renewal. With each page turned, you may find solace in the power of forgiveness and boundless depths of true love.

And yet, there was something else there, hidden beneath the layers of hurt—a glimmer of hope. Hope that perhaps, despite all the pain, they could still find their way back to each other. That maybe, just maybe, love would be enough to heal the wounds they both carried.

Their eyes remained locked for what felt like an eternity, and in that silent exchange, they said more to each other than words ever could. The world outside faded away, leaving just the two of them, suspended in a fragile moment of understanding.

Without thinking, Kabir reached out, his hand gently brushing against hers. His touch was light, hesitant, but Siya didn't pull away. She let their fingers linger together, and though they didn't speak, they both felt it—the connection that had always been there, the one that had never truly disappeared, no matter how hard life had tried to break it.

The car slowed as it neared Siya's street, and Kabir hesitated before speaking. "Can we get off here?" he asked softly, his voice barely breaking the quiet. "I… I'd like to walk with you."

Siya glanced at him, her eyes softening, and after a brief pause, she nodded. The driver pulled over a little further from her house, and they both stepped out into the cool night air.

The lane stretched ahead of them, lined with dimly lit streetlights and the occasional chirp of crickets breaking the stillness. Kabir and Siya walked side by side, their pace slow and deliberate. Neither of them spoke at first, content to simply be near each other for a little while longer, the sound of their footsteps echoing in the night.

As they walked, Kabir stole glances at her, feeling the tension between them slowly unravel. The walk felt like an extension of their earlier silent conversation, a way to prolong the moment, to give them both a little more time.

Siya, though quiet, felt a strange sense of peace. She didn't know what the future held for them, but she knew that they were both trying—both searching for a way back to each other. And somehow, that was enough.

As they neared her home, Kabir stopped, turning to face her fully. His eyes, now soft and full of emotion, held hers once more. "Thank you… for walking with me," he whispered.

Siya smiled faintly, a quiet understanding passing between them. They weren't fixed, not yet. But for now, they were on the right path. Together.

Siya glanced over at Kabir, her heart swelling with a mix of emotions. She had waited so long for this—for him to come back to her, not just physically, but with his heart fully open. After a few moments of silence, she spoke softly, her voice steady but filled with meaning. "Even if you weren't near, Kabir, you were always with me. No matter the distance or the silence, I would've waited a lifetime for you."

Kabir stopped walking for a moment, her words hitting him like a wave. He turned to face her, the streetlights casting a soft glow on her face. He could see the sincerity in her eyes, the depth of her love and the patience she had shown him despite everything. He took a deep breath, his voice low but filled with emotion.

"Siya," he began, "whatever is mine, I hand it over to you. My heart, my soul... everything. It's all yours." He reached for her hand, holding it gently, as if it were something precious. "I've seen the world now, more than I ever thought I would. But you know what I realized?" He paused, his voice thick with realization. "It's all a sham. All the distractions, the noise, the so-called excitement. None of it means anything. You... you're the only truth I've ever known."

Siya's breath caught in her throat. She had waited for this—for him to understand, to see her for who she was and what she had always been for him. Her eyes glistened with unshed tears, not of sadness but of overwhelming love.

"And I know this now," Kabir continued, stepping closer to her, his thumb gently brushing the back of her hand. "If I'm the wall that supports everything between us, you're the ceiling that protects it from the storms, from the rain, from everything that could bring it down." His voice softened, full of tenderness. "Together, we're home, Siya. You and me."

Siya felt the warmth of his words wrap around her like a blanket. She had always believed in them, in the love they shared, even when he had been too blind to see it. Now, hearing him speak so vulnerably, so openly, she knew that everything had been worth it.

They began walking again, the quiet of the night settling around them. Siya leaned into Kabir slightly, her arm brushing against his. "I never needed grand gestures or promises," she

---

The Amaranthine Promises: Where love finds its way in the labyrinth of fate, illuminating the path to redemption and renewal. With each page turned, you may find solace in the power of forgiveness and boundless depths of true love.

whispered, her voice steady. "All I ever needed was for you to see me, to see us, and to fight for it the way I did."

Kabir nodded, his grip on her hand tightening just a little. "I see it now, Siya. I see everything clearly. And I'm not letting go. Not ever."

As they continued on the path, Kabir paused mid-step, his hand slipping into his pocket as they neared Siya's door. His fingers closed around something familiar, something he'd been carrying with him for weeks now. He hesitated for a moment, feeling the weight of the moment—the significance of what he was about to do. Siya looked at him, curiosity flickering in her eyes.

"There's something I need to give you," Kabir said quietly, his voice trembling just a little. He pulled out a neatly folded piece of paper, worn at the edges from being carried around for so long. "I've been meaning to give this to you since the day I left. I didn't know how, or when the right time would come. But... I think now is the moment."

Siya stared at the letter in his hands, her heart beating a little faster. She didn't know what to expect, but there was something about the way he was holding it, with such care, that made her feel like this wasn't just a letter. It was more than that—it was his heart on paper.

He unfolded it slowly, handing it to her. "Read it, Siya. Please."

Siya's fingers trembled slightly as she took the letter from him. She opened it, her eyes moving across the words, her breath catching in her throat as she read. Every word was like a piece of him that she hadn't seen before— every sentence, an admission of the depth of his love and regret.

The letter read:

"I wonder if horror movies were so scary if, I wasn't watching them with you...

I wonder if the food would taste as good if, you weren't the one cooking it for me...

I wonder if the night sky would be so beautiful if, we weren't looking at it together...

I wonder if music would be as romantic if, we weren't sharing our earphones, listening to our favourite songs together...

I wonder if dancing would be as much fun if, we weren't swaying to the rhythm of our favourite songs...

I wonder if long drives would be as exciting if, you weren't sitting beside me, making every turn feel like an adventure...

I wonder if the mornings would be as bright and beautiful if, I wasn't waking up anticipating our meetings...

I wonder if shopping would be as entertaining if, I wasn't carrying your bags and pretending to complain...

And finally, I wonder if life would be life at all if, you weren't in it with me...

I can't imagine my life without you. I'm sorry, Siya. For everything. I've been an idiot—a total fool—and I know I probably always will be in some ways. I'll still do silly things, and I'll probably annoy you with my stupidity, but I promise you this: I'll never do anything to break your heart again. I love you, Siya. I've always loved you. And I always will."

Siya finished reading, her eyes misting over as she looked up at him. Kabir was standing there, his eyes searching hers, nervousness painted across his face. It was the most vulnerable she had ever seen him—no bravado, no mask, just Kabir, stripped of everything but his love for her.

For a moment, there was nothing but silence between them, the night holding its breath. Then, Siya spoke, her voice soft but steady. "You really are an idiot, you know that?" she said, but there was no anger, no hurt— just affection. She stepped closer to him, folding the letter back and holding it against her chest.

Kabir's heart raced, unsure of what was to come. He nodded, smiling sheepishly. "Yeah, I know. But I'm your idiot, right?"

Siya chuckled, shaking her head, the tension between them dissolving in that moment. "You've always been my idiot, Kabir. Even when you hurt me, even when you pushed me away, you were still mine."

He reached for her hand, holding it gently. "I'm sorry for all of it, Siya. For letting my ego get in the way. For making you feel like you didn't matter. I was blind. And I know I can't undo the past, but I want to make it right. I want to be the man who deserves you, who stands by your side, not just as your lover, but as your partner. In everything."

Siya felt a warmth flood her chest, a sense of peace she hadn't felt in so long. She looked into his eyes, seeing the sincerity in them, the raw vulnerability. "I don't need perfection, Kabir. I never did. I just needed you to see me, to see us, and to fight for us. And I believe you now. I believe you're ready to fight."

He stepped closer, his forehead resting gently against hers. "I'll fight for you every day, Siya. Every single day."

In that quiet moment, under the blanket of stars and the dim streetlights, Kabir leaned in. With all the emotions of the past weeks, months—the love, the regret, the hope—he kissed her. Not a rushed, desperate kiss, but something tender and full of promise. His lips brushed against her forehead first, a gesture of respect, of apology, before they moved softly to hers.

It was a kiss that spoke of new beginnings, of healing, and of a love that had weathered the storm. A kiss that said, "I'm here. I've always been here, and I always will be."

When they finally pulled apart, Siya smiled softly, her eyes still glistening with unshed tears. "You know," she said playfully, "life isn't going to be easy with you, is it?"

Kabir grinned, his eyes twinkling. "Probably not. But I promise, it'll never be boring."

They both laughed, the sound echoing through the empty street, and in that moment, everything felt right again. Together, they started walking toward Siya's home, hand in hand, ready to face whatever came next. Because now, they knew—they were home, as long as they had each other.

The Amaranthine Promises: Where love finds its way in the labyrinth of fate, illuminating the path to redemption and renewal. With each page turned, you may find solace in the power of forgiveness and boundless depths of true love.

In the end, Kabir realized that the universe had conspired not to break him but to guide him toward his true destiny. Siya was his beacon of hope, a love so deep that it healed wounds from the past long buried in the shadows of regret. With her by his side, the pieces of his heart once shattered by betrayal found their way back together. Every promise, every smile, every shared silence became a testament to the life they had reclaimed, the dreams they had resurrected from the ashes. The echoes of their journey, full of pain and perseverance, whispered that this love was different, a love built on trust, respect, and second chances. And as Kabir held Siya close, he knew that what had once been lost in the chaos of Maya was now found, stronger than ever, in the arms of Siya.

They continued down the sidewalk, their steps in sync, as if they were moving to the rhythm of a song only they could hear. As they neared Siya's home, there was a quiet contentment between them, the kind that only comes from knowing that, no matter what storms they had weathered, they had found their way back to each other.

Underneath the streetlights, with the world quiet and still around them, they knew that they had come home—together.

In the radiant glow of love's dazzling dawn, Kabir and Siya emerge from the darkness of their past, united in their shared journey of redemption and renewal. With each step forward, they embrace the promise of a future filled with boundless love and infinite possibility, guided by the unwavering light of their shared destiny.

The Amaranthine Promises: Where love finds its way in the labyrinth of fate, illuminating the path to redemption and renewal. With each page turned, you may find solace in the power of forgiveness and boundless depths of true love.

Moral

The journey of love is not always easy, but it is in the moments of struggle and adversity that we discover our true strength and resilience. Healing takes time, and sometimes, the pain of the past can pave the way for a future filled with hope and fulfilment. Love that is meant to be will always find its way, even if it takes a detour through heartache. Forgiveness, trust, and the courage to open your heart again are the keys to rediscovering happiness. In the end, the love we cherish most is often found after we've learned to let go of what once broke us.

A Glimpse into Tomorrow

On a picturesque morning, sunlight streaming through the windows of a cozy, yet elegant home. Laughter echoes through the hallways—carefree, warm, and full of life. A little girl runs across the room, her giggles filling the air as she's chased by none other than Kabir, his face alight with playful mischief.

"Gotcha!" Kabir laughs as he scoops his daughter up in his arms, spinning her around while she squeals with joy.

In the background, Siya watches with a smile that says more than words ever could. There's a calmness in her now, the kind that only comes from the peace of building a life with someone you love, despite all the hurdles they once faced. She leans against the kitchen counter, casually sipping her morning coffee, watching the love of her life and their little one with an expression that could only be described as pure contentment.

But there's something more here—something bubbling beneath the surface. Kabir and Siya are no longer just two individuals finding their way through love. They are partners, navigating the thrilling and unpredictable journey of marriage. There are moments of sheer joy, like this one, but also moments that test their strength, challenge their understanding of each other, and push them to redefine what love and family truly mean.

What's to come?

- A suitcase lies open on the bed, clothes spilling out of it. A boarding pass for Paris pokes out of a pocket, hinting at adventures waiting beyond the horizon. Kabir and Siya exchange a look—half excitement, half exhaustion—as they juggle travel plans, work meetings, and parenting.

- Kabir in a boardroom, his gaze intense, navigating the challenges of his growing career. But somewhere in the midst of all that, his phone buzzes with a picture of Siya and their daughter. He pauses, his face softening, reminded of the life he's built and the anchor that grounds him.

- Siya, successful in her own right, taking charge at work. But even in the midst of her achievements, she sneaks a glance at her phone—a picture of Kabir and their daughter at a park. She smiles, balancing her ambitions and her love for the family they've created.

Now, back to a quiet night. The family is seated on a couch, the little girl fast asleep between them. Kabir and Siya sit in comfortable silence, hands intertwined. And as the world outside slows down, they steal a glance at each other—a silent promise that no matter what life throws at them, they'll face it together.

But this isn't the end—oh no, this is just the beginning of their next chapter.

From building a strong family foundation to experiencing the joy and chaos of parenting, to traveling the world and finding success in both their personal and professional lives, Kabir and Siya's story is far from over. The challenges they'll face as a married couple, the new adventures that await, and the love that continues to evolve—this is where their journey truly begins.

"And what happens next?"

Well, that's a story for another time. But trust me, it's going to be filled with more love, laughter, drama, and surprises than ever before.

Stay tuned… the next chapter of their lives is just around the corner.

Thank you!

I want to express my deepest gratitude to the three incredible women in my life—my guiding lights, my "lady luck." To my beautiful wife, who has stood by me through every storm and every triumph, your love and unwavering support have been my greatest fortune. To my lovely daughter, who has brought so much luck, joy, and happiness into my world, you remind me daily of the beauty and blessings in life. And to my mom, whose strength, wisdom, and sacrifices have made me who I am today—I owe every success to the foundation you've built for me. Just as the women in my book anchor the story, these three remarkable women have anchored my life, and for that, I am eternally grateful.

Disclaimer

This book is a work of fiction. Names, characters, businesses, places, events, and incidents are either the products of the author's imagination or are used in a fictitious manner. Any resemblance to actual persons, living or dead, or actual events is purely coincidental.

The author has made every effort to ensure that no individual, organization, or entity is identifiable in this story. Any similarities between the characters, events, or places described in this book and real individuals or events are purely coincidental and unintended.

While this book may draw inspiration from certain life experiences, the characters and scenarios are fictionalized. Names, traits, and situations have been altered and re-imagined, and no actual names or identities of individuals, places, or entities have been used. Any reference to real-life individuals, whether intentional or unintentional, is purely fictional and should not be construed as factual.

This work is not intended to defame, harm, or malign any individual, community, religious group, or organization. The beliefs, thoughts, and actions of the characters in this book are fictional and do not reflect the author's personal views, beliefs, or opinions.

The author has taken all reasonable precautions to avoid any unintentional infringement on the intellectual property of others. Any similarities between this book and other works are purely coincidental.

The content of this book is original, and no part has been knowingly copied or adapted from any other publication. Furthermore, no legal action should be taken against the author or the publisher based on perceived resemblances to actual people, events, or organizations.

The author disclaims all liability for any harm, damages, or misunderstandings that may arise from reading this book.

The content in this book is meant solely for entertainment and creative expression. It should not be used as a basis for legal disputes or complaints.

About the Author

Ronak Barvaliya

Ronak embarked on his professional journey in the financial industry at a remarkably young age, building an illustrious career that spans over 18 years. Alongside his professional achievements, Ronak has always nurtured a deep passion for storytelling, writing short blogs, and delving into the world of books.

It was only recently that Ronak discovered his ability to write a full-length book—a realization born from his desire to inspire hope in a world that often feels overwhelming.

Through his writing, he seeks to remind readers that life offers second chances, that love lost does not signify the end, and that true love always finds its way back. His mission is to instil belief in the power of love, the magic of fairy tales, and the inherent goodness within people.

Beyond writing, Ronak is an avid traveller who finds joy in exploring new places and cultures. He cherishes moments playing snooker with his friends, enjoys the thrill of cricket and swimming, and shares a profound connection with music, which he believes is the very essence of his soul. Deeply spiritual, Ronak values prayers and blessings, which he considers guiding forces in his life.

Through his work, Ronak aspires to touch hearts, ignite hope, and remind readers of the beauty in holding on to love and faith, no matter how challenging life gets.